HV McDermott was born in England in the station hotel Spennymoor, County Durham. At the age of six, she came to live in Roscommon. She now lives with her husband, Batty, and seven children under the shadow of the Curlew Mountains on the eastern shore of Lough Gara.

Dedicated to my Bartholomew McDermott and my wonderful family and friends.

HV McDermott

SILENCE OF SNOW

AUSTIN MACAULEY PUBLISHERS™

LONDON • CAMBRIDGE • NEW YORK • SHARJAH

A CIP catalogue record for this title is available from the British Library.

ISBN 9781788486835 (Paperback)
ISBN 9781788486842 (Hardback)
ISBN 9781788486859 (E-Book)

www.austinmacauley.com

First Published (2018)
Austin Macauley Publishers Ltd
25 Canada Square
Canary Wharf
London
E14 5LQ

For my Batty and seven children, Shaun, Joseph, Sharon, Tara, Hilda, Michael and Lisa; and 16 grandchildren.

Table of Contents

The Leaving

The sun was shining, and the air was warm with the sweet smells of autumn harvesting time. It was probably Michael John Finns favourite time of the year, with the Meitheals and the parties afterwards that sometimes went on all night. He loved the show in Boyle every year, looking forward to the craic of switching tags on produce and cattle, then correcting them again just to get the auld fellas hopping mad. The show dances were great for getting the older women out dancing nice and close, but he, never having known his own mother, thought the young lads were awful for not giving their mothers a dance.

He left the small provincial town, unimportant and forgotten, with the sweep of the Curlew Mountains rising up behind it, and the pleasant shops and houses ringing around the Crescent. He drove his father's old Prefect car through the streets of Boyle, his childhood friend and comrade Tommy Lee by his side. In the back seat lay his old navy blue Crombie coat and battered suitcase, and he had left home with no blessing from his father.

That morning after an hour's sleep, he had awaked with a headache and a bad taste in his mouth. He needed a short rest as he was driving to Youghal, the arrangements being, he was driving down and a cousin would return the car to his father in a day or so. He felt this dark inward unhappiness like a septic limb, black and swollen, settling in him. The wrench of leaving was a lot tougher than he had imagined. Coming up to the kitchen for a cup of tea, he was full of gloom looking at this father crouched in the fireside chair, fully dressed but unshaven and hair uncombed. He started to talk to Michael John, but his words were directed to his shoes as much as to him.

His father had never forgiven him for coming into the world the night his poor mother left it. So it fell to Aunt Maggie to rear him, and he loved her so. Maggie had given up her good job as a seamstress in an up-and-coming firm in Dublin, to come back to the West to take care of her beautiful sister's child and to keep house for her brother-in-law, Paul Finn.

Maggie never thought it was any hardship, as she loved her pretty young sister dearly. She knew Paul Finn all her life and they had made a beautiful couple. The whole world could see that Paul worshipped his young, beautiful, kind and gentle wife, and that she in return loved him dearly. Paul had tried over the years to warm to his young son, failing miserably – maybe if he had looked more like his mother; but no, he was the image of himself.

It was Our Lady's day, the fifteenth of August; Maggie had gone with a busload early to Knock. It was an annual pilgrimage, normally with her friend Maureen in her car. She would miss seeing him actually leave, but he knew she could not bear to see him go, and this was a deliberate change of plan. She had told him last night that she would pray for strength for all of them, especially his father. *"I know you think he has no feelings for you, but I can see him looking at you when he thinks you are not looking; tears come to his eyes, and embarrassment. He leaves the room, but not because he does not want to be in the same room as you, quite the opposite. I know he feels guilty for the way he treated you; it is not what your dear mother would have wished him to do. He loved her dearly, he grieved for a long time after her death; it was unhealthy, but how do you tell a man to stop grieving the wife he loved. I did tell him some time back that he should say he was sorry for the way he treated you, or rather mistreated you. He just shook his head and said it was years too late for that now. He had not known it was happening for a long time; by then, he said you were fully grown and needed him no more.*

"He always gave me more than I needed to get you the best of things in life, but he never gave you what you really wanted. I hope he gets the courage to speak up before you go." She said, *"She understood it was not healthy to stay with this kind of atmosphere in the house and placed a brown Scapular of the Sacred Heart and a linen hanky with fifty pounds, probably the only money she had in the world in his hand."* Michael John refused; she laughed, *"Now when you have made your fortune and are a rich man sure, I know you will remember your Aunt Maggie."* Punching him playfully, she smiled. *"Do you remember the fur coat that the posh one home from America staying in Lee's was wearing one Christmas, you would have been about thirteen, and I was after a bout of the flu, I was shivering at mass. You promised to buy me one when you grew up, saying I would never be cold again! Well, I'll be waiting,"* she said with a chuckle. *"Don't forget, I want to be able to lose my hand in the fur."*

Michael John watched his aunt as she went to ready the tea and thought to himself she seems to have shrunk a couple of feet the last couple of months since the arrangements for America had started. Her face had lost its rosy complexion that was always so evident in summer time. She loved helping outside with the hay, raking and making the rows into head cocks of hay or twisting hay to make ropes to hold the head of the haycocks down. She didn't run from the bog work either, loving the outdoors, but the affectionate name of Rosy that they teasingly called her at home, didn't suit anymore. She had asked Michael John to bring her to the doctors a number of times, but when asked of any results, her answer was always the same: *"I am grand."*

Queen of the May

Nelly Lee was a very beautiful girl, with chestnut brown hair falling in cascades down her shoulders and back, and the bluest eyes – actually piercing blue – so unusual for red hair. She was loved by the entire neighbourhood. Her beauty was not just skin deep. She cared about all around her, every human being and animals as well. She missed her brother, Frank, when he emigrated; he was some years older than her and had always taken care of her being the youngest. He was doing so well in England and had great English friends looking out for him that took the sting out of missing him.

The lady of the big house, where her brother worked, came from an old established millionaire family, still leading in the business. Bolts of material in every new colour or design – silks, satin, lace, cotton or linen – were sent to her ladyship. Once her wishes or needs were fulfilled, be it a cotton or lace, the remainder was then taken out of the sewing room and left in the staff room. The staff were allowed to share the ends as they wished. Frank's mother was a gifted seamstress, on an old second-hand sewing machine she had received for her eighteenth birthday. Frank started sending material over and Nelly was in her element making dresses, skirts, coats and tops for her beautiful daughter.

A song contest was being arranged for June the twenty-sixth as part of a concert in the parochial hall. There were to be prizes in several different categories, and Nelly was looking forward to it excitedly. She had been told often enough that she had a voice of a linnet.

It was an overcast afternoon, the morning rain still clinging to the turnip leaves; as Nelly lifted her head, she could hear the corncrake hoarsely repeating what sounded like "*egg and bacon, egg and bacon*". It was a boring job, thinning turnips, but today it was no problem; it was the twenty-fifth of May, tomorrow was the big night.

Money had arrived from her brother in the morning's post, enough for a new pair of shoes to match the lovely dress her mother had made for the occasion. Her thoughts kept fleeting back to the neighbour, Paul Lavin, who she had feelings for. Was he the one who was going to walk her home after the concert in front of her friends! Her father had asked her to thin the half ridge of young turnips as the weather suited. He had to go to town in the trap to pay the rates, and her mother went along to buy those pair of pearl-coloured shoes, with slight heel to match the dress she had made for her. *"I will buy you a Peggy's Leg to sweeten your voice,"* he winked, as he walked out the door. Closing the door behind her, Nelly went down to the tillage. Working away, Nelly flew along the ridges, humming to herself, trying to forget the pain in her back from bending; all she could think of was to get home and have some honey for her throat. *'So much happiness,'* she thought to herself she was the luckiest girl alive, if only things could have stayed like that forever.

Next moment, she found herself being flung into the furrow of the ridge, onto her back, every breath of air in her lungs being thrown out of her. A heavy, smelly weight upon her, Nelly felt smothered and a sharp cracked button was causing a pain in her neck. Never having been treated harshly in her life, she now felt in mortal danger. She could hear the children playing in the schoolyard, but with the pressure on her throat, no one could hear her. This mad thing tore away at her clothes, she was powerless to stop him, the smell of sweat in her nostrils, the cry in her throat stifled by the big calloused hand across her mouth, with her hands pinned to her chest, and he raped her. When it was over, she saw it was Hugh Drury, a vile neighbour she disliked, but was never afraid of until now. Looking down on her, he spluttered, *"You brought this on yourself, with your fancy clothes and singing away like a slut."*

A long time seemed to have passed before Nelly rose out of the furrow, standing shaking, her brain fluttering in every direction. Pulling her torn clothes tightly, she ran home and slammed the door. Moments later, she ran out again to the cow house, and brought in the tin bath. She spent the next hour collecting water from the flash at the end of the horse shed, and dragged loads of sticks in for the boiling pan of water and locked the door again. Picking up a large lump of sunlight soap, Nelly started to scrub. And when she threw out the suds down the gully outside the front door, her old life went too.

Going up to her attic bedroom, she sat down to think; there was no one to turn for help. She would have to keep it to herself, yet anyway. Hugh Drury was a man of means. His father had left him a fine farm, plus what could be called a gentleman's residence with coach house, horse shed, and a clutter of other outhouses. It wasn't just that, he was a man, and people would say she encouraged him.

Remembering her friend, Mary Ann Lenihan, who all her life had wanted to be a nun and help people. Her dream was to go abroad, to work with the poor in Africa after taking her final vows. She had spoken to the Reverend Mother of the order she wished to join, and the Reverend Mother had told her to take grinds in English, as you needed a good foundation in the entrance examination. So she made arrangements to work for a local teacher, doing chores and cleaning both school and his home. Making meals was also one of the chores and after washing up, they would start the grinds. Now Master Leo Tansey was a tall, likable man, held in respect by the locals.

Mary Ann was very pleased with her progress and on the night before taking her entrance exam, she brought him a bottle of whiskey. As Mary was making the tea, the Master kept nibbling at the whiskey and kept referring to The Last Supper. When she called to say it was ready, he came in bleary eyed, grabbed hold of Mary, and raped her. Afterwards, he asked her to marry him. She just ran; no one could find her for days. Ten days later, she was found sitting frozen to death with her hands clasped in prayer, beside the grotto of Saint Bernadette on the other side of the mountain. Nelly had heard people, both men and women, blame poor Mary, even though the Master admitted to what he had done. So it was he who got sympathy, and Mary got the grave; the doctor thought Mary died head in hands from the shock.

Eventually, her mother returned from town to see her beautiful, gentle daughter in shock and disarray, a far cry from how she normally looked, like some tender glasshouse flower blooming accidently amid the harder natives of the field. Now she looked at her daughter with some trepidation, knowing something bad had befallen her and fearing the worst. She sat down to hear Nelly's heart-rending story, and though she asked, Nelly would not divulge his name. Subduing her own feelings in her need to help her daughter, they formulated a plan. She wrote to her older sister, Peggie Lee, who lived in Co Clare. Peggie had a wee cake shop which did good business. Arrangements were swiftly made for Nelly to come to her, and both would help each other. If anyone questioned, the story was that Peggie was under the weather and needed help, Nelly would be helping. Nelly would go to night school to learn shorthand and typing. Poor Nelly's fate was sealed.

The Lee Family

Nelly's brother, Bernard, went to England on the boat, with two lads from Cuppanagh who had jobs waiting for them, and hoped to talk the boss into a job for Bernard. With Bernard's first taste of real freedom and loneliness in equal doses, he started drinking the minute he left shore. Later on, at maybe four in the morning when the lads went to bed, Bernard went back up on deck to get some fresh air as the night was calm. The night air was chilly and with no light to see in any direction, he fell asleep on a bench on the bow side. Six o'clock came and went, all passengers disembarked along with the two lads. The boys hung around for an hour, and while people milled all around them, decided to go for the train, as they knew Bernard had the address in Leeds in his pocket.

A cleaning crew form the North Wall came aboard and found Bernard fast asleep on the bench. Being woken up from a fuzzed and drunken sleep, he was unable to understand the accents. After repeating themselves many times, he realised where he was and how he came to be there. Up he got, said *"Good luck"* and headed down to find his battered suitcase. It was miraculously where he had left it, under the seat he had been drinking on. Picking it up, he slowly made his way out and down the gang plank, his spirits down too. On the quays, Bernard searched for the boys, cursing them and his own stupidity in equal measures.

Tired and nursing the mother of all hangovers, he sat and watched the loading and unloading going on. Looking around, he spotted a strangely dressed fellow holding a magnificent Chestnut by the bridle; on the other side of the traces, a black stallion stood with his head held high as if of noble birth. Bernard loved horses; at home, he had been known as the horse whisperer. Admiring the fabulous beasts, he daydreamed about one day owing such magnificent animals.

A tugboat pulling in along the quay tooted, making puffing sounds, unnerving the black horse; it reared up on his hind legs pulling the man, the chestnut horse and the carriage towards the Irish Sea. Bernard leaped from his seat on the old case and raced like lightening towards the scene, talking all the time as he ran alongside to the black stallion. A few seconds later, Bernard reached him, grabbing the reins. The black one, still neighing and stomping his hooves, foaming at the mouth, fixed his gaze on Bernard who was soothingly talking to him, and keeping eye contact; slowly, he settled down and came to a standstill.

The coach door screeched open and a very shaken but well-dressed man alighted, grabbing Bernard by the arms as he still held the black stallion by the reins. Speaking with a posh accent, he asked Bernard his name and where he came from. Bernard gave him his name telling him he was new off the boat, that he was a carpenter by trade, but had a great love for horses. The man nodded, *"I can see that for myself and the horse seems to reciprocate those feelings." Thanks to you, we have all had a very lucky escape."*

He handed him a twenty pound note; Bernard refused saying, *"Anyone would have done the same."*

The gentleman stepped forward saying, *"But no one else did, I insist you accept, and I would like to offer you employment."* From the authority in the gentleman's voice, Bernard knew better than to argue, and before he knew what was happening, he had the money in his pocket and was sitting in the nicely furnished carriage thinking, *'I must write to the lads and tell them of my good luck and fortune as soon as I reach this gent's house.'*

They had been travelling for about an hour when they pulled up in front of this huge house. This was on a grandeur, bigger than anything Bernard had seen back home. The gentleman went to alight and turned to Bernard saying, *"The black horse is known as 'Lee' so I will call you Bernard."* He then called the driver over instructing him to: *"Bring Bernard around to the back kitchen and have Smith feed him, and to get Patterson to make up a bed for him under the east turret,"* disappearing in through the front door, out of sight. The driver, Lloyd, told him as they set off for the back door that he had fallen on his feet. *"The master is after giving you a room left for guests, during the hunting season. Now mate, I don't begrudge you one bit, I know I owe you my life, not least my job and anytime I can help you, I will be there for you."* Then they entered the kitchen and he issued Smith with the master's orders, indicating to Bernard to sit on the chair beside the fire and in great detail he held them all in awe, as he regaled them with the story of Bernard the Irishman, calling him the 'Horse Whisperer'.

Return from Cork

One year later, Nelly returned from Cork. Her mother went to town with the trap to collect Nelly from the train. Everyone knew they were a close, loving family. But the reunion between mother and daughter was electric in the eyes of the people looking on.

Nelly was asked how her aunt was, and how pale she looked herself. Lying didn't come easy to Nelly. So she honestly felt her aunt improved immensely. She had taken a young, cheerful country girl to her house; she was excellent with food and people, giving Peggie time for herself, and time for her to visit her friend. So it worked out grand for both of them.

On returning home, Nelly stayed home with her parents each night. No one could understand, she was such a fun-loving person. Neighbours come to the conclusion that she must be following her sister Kathleen into the convent.

Hardly a year passed, again the neighbourhood was in a swirl with rumours. Word was that Nelly was marrying Hugh Drury during the eleven o'clock mass in the half parish. Nelly fell from grace, toppled off that pedestal they had placed her on, to end up very low, saying she is just after money and prestige, the house twice the size of any house around and a hundred plus acres of fine land. The house was not surrounded with buildings of cow houses, pig houses, calf houses, dairy, turf shed, horse shed, large hay shed and an avenue up from the road, graced with beech trees on each side, with daffodils waving to and fro.

Nelly felt she was in the way of her brother John's happiness. He had a strong line with a local girl, so if she went, they could marry into the house. So she turned around and said *"Yes"* when Drury asked her to marry him.

Well, you couldn't say he asked; all he said was, *"No one else would marry her, her being second-hand goods."* As if he was innocent, but she felt if she married him, she would be able to after Tommie's inheritance if he ever came back looking for her.

Tom the Milk Man

The first year or so, life with the tyrant was bearable enough. Old Tommy Cane, the milkman, was a regular visitor to the house. Now Tom was a wee bit innocent, not much as one meeting first time would notice, but he fell for everything people told him, he was terribly good-natured. His mother, Maggie, thought the sun, stars and moon shone out of her Tom. She was near blind, was allowed a small bit of weekly money and a free radio. She professed daily that she may have little sight but she had a wonderful life thanks to her son and daughter – Tom lived with his mother and sister, Nancy. His sister did all the work around the small farm, even spraying the potatoes. Tom ploughed and mowed the meadow, Nancy did everything else mind.

Although in summertime, Tom was all day long on the road, sometimes late into the night, depending where he ended in the queue. Some smart fellow might send Tom on an errand; on returning, they could have ten or twelve carts to empty. She also worshipped her brother. Every second house sent him for messages, be it cigarettes, sugar, butter, batteries for radio, though not many bothered him with radios, as they were far and few between. He never wrote anything down, but was never known to forget anyone.

As he called up to the dairy door – always had – instead of the tyrant bringing it down to the roadside probably a half mile, Tom had brought messages for the tyrant's mother. But then she was a gracious soul. She would always have a bit for him to eat, after his ten mile round trip on Molly, his grey mare. Then Ellie was a wonderful cook; she had worked in The Royal Hotel as a cook for ten years. Her

Uncle Mathias owned the place. He brought notes from his mother, and left them under the can of paraffin oil that Tom brought on his way home from the creamery. Nelly had continued having something ready for him to eat, as Tom would be about half way home, Molly would have a drink of water and a bit of a rest.

It was a miserable, wet and windy day; the poor old hens were having the eggs knocked out of them. They were been blown all over the place, so Nelly decided to put them in their shed and tie a few sheaves of oats up on to the roost to keep them warm and safe. Nelly was in the oats shed, bending down to take out a sheaf of oats, when a rat jumped out of the straw and took a bite on to her throat – held on with great grip.

With the wind blowing, Tom shouted "*Hello*"; on hearing no answer, he went into the shed. Seeing her predicament, he pulled the rat off and went ahead to suck the poison. Having spat out a couple of times, in walked the tyrant and saw them together, bending down; he picked up the pick that was left behind the door, lifting it up over his head. Nelly pushed in between them screaming, showing him the wound the rat had made. Grabbing hold of a lump of ivy that grew through the small shed window, she was able to shove him away.

The tyrant then threw down the pick in the channel; he began screaming at Tom, *"Never come near my house again,"* forgetting that Tom had only been obliging him all these years, really out of respect for his good mother, God have mercy on her, she never could understand her youngest son, although always made excuses for him. Her three older boys, one more so than the other, were kinder and well liked than the other; as each left the country, the neighbourhood grieved for them with her.

Her Jim always said, *"There was a throwback every family, each having a black sheep."* Maybe the legends about black Drury in the eighteenth century must have some credence. It was the black look on Hugh's face that bothered

24

his parents, the must and how it was always someone else's fault, not his. Once he hung a dog prince, because he chased a cow the wrong way when it was his fault for giving the wrong command. Now, he would have to wheel the creamery cans down to the road. Three cans in early meant three goes to the road; well of course, Nelly would have to do it.

Before Eoin's Birth

Much to Nelly's amazement, after a few years of marriage, she found herself pregnant. Nelly succumbed to his advances as a wife should, but she could never blot the memories of the rape from her mind. Mercifully, it was always swift and Hugh would immediately go to sleep, snoring loudly enough to rattle the rafters.

The morning sunlight streamed through Nelly's small bedroom window board of her new home. St Patrick's was nearing, Nelly saw some beautiful shamrock in the corner beside the well, as she pulled up a bucket of spring water. Bending down to pick some, she fell out of her standing into a heap on the ground. The next thing she knew, she was laying on her own bed and the tyrant leaving a mug of steaming tea on the butter box, at the bedside. He grunted, *"Are you sick."*

"No, I am pregnant," she said. After resting a while, she went up to the kitchen, a fire blazed licking the black pot on a crane where porridge was being made. Saying nothing, he placed two bowls on the table, one in front of her usual seat. That was the first kindness he had ever shown her, apart from mood swings when he would take off out of the house. For the next six months, Nelly had knitted and sewed, and had a general feeling of wellbeing bordering normality. One day, she asked him to bring her a load of willows from the bog field, which he did the very next day. Nelly placed them in a drain behind the house; she loved making beautiful things out of the willows. Lovingly, she created a Moses basket fit for a prince.

When the tyrant saw it, he grunted and went off to town. Around a month later, he came home from town and landed into the kitchen with a beautiful carved cradle. *"For when the weather gets cold,"* he grunted. Nelly smiled to herself; as a rule, a baby did not get a bed until he was born, the Moses basket had been holding clothes. Nelly had lost all superstitions three years before. Well health while Nelly enjoyed good health. Apart from milking three cows and taking the cream for butter in the dairy, her time was her own. On nearing the eighth month, making it the middle of November, Nelly went out as usual to milk the black poly cow, as now Polly was the only one to milk. She found a new glass churn with a handle on the table in the dairy. This meant she could sit down on a creel and churn away to make the butter, which she found great as her ankles could swell up, when they felt like it.

It was a starry night and the ground was covered with crunchy snow. Nelly was listening to 'Hark, now hear the angels sing' on Radio Éireann, when she let out a scream. Actually it was the fear, after all she had gone through the last three years when Tommie was born and taken without a word or otherwise. The tyrant leapt like a scalded cat and ran out the door. It was then the real fear set in. In fifteen minutes, her mother was by her side and holding her hand soothingly. In what seemed a short time, horses' hooves clattering on the cobblestones could be heard ringing outside. In the backdoor, Maggie Maughan came floating with her large rosy face and wide girth belying her weight, as she glided along the kitchen floor towards Nelly. Leaving her bag of accoutrements on the floor, she took Nelly's hand.

She was the most important person in the parish; she had trained as a nurse and midwife in England. She had come back to take care of her aging parents, after the last brother went to America. She was a great daughter, giving health care, company and every act of kindness a child could bestow on her gentle parents. After her last parent went to their eternal reward, she took to traverse the countryside doing good deeds. From midwife, helping the sick, her hands were always ready to help, even station preparations which had been important to people, to have the house as clean as possible, to bring the mass into their homes. Her other main act was the laying out of fond neighbour's mortal remains.

She did not have to knock on any door, she would pull over the latch and shout, *"God bless all here."* As a rule leaving, she would say, *"God bless the cow,"* after receiving some milk. Now Maggie was no oil painting, she had a long horsey, rosy red face. A long beaky nose with a large brown wart on the side of it; her long lanky grey hair had a hard hat pulled down over the ears. I believe if you asked anyone who knew her, they would swear she was beautiful, everyone seemed so full of love for the woman. She was revered as doctor in the community. So when she brought a healthy son into the world, and placed him gently into Nelly's arms, then wiping her face, the smile Maggie got was surely the look of worship.

Joy Knows No Bounds

No one in the neighbourhood had ever understood why Nelly Lee had married Hugh Drury. No one knew of the rape and her baby given up for adoption. Many a fine well-to-do lads in the locality and the next parish would have married Nelly in a heartbeat. Nelly's feelings of guilt and shame won out; she wished she had no baggage, and that she could have accepted the affections of one fine young lad, but it was hard to get him to understand. They had some great laughs together and liked the same songs and poetry. She knew it would be not fair on anyone to tell the truth, so Nelly could not share her secret with anyone outside the family. She felt if she married him, she would be able to look after her son's inheritances for the day he would hopefully come looking for her.

Nelly gave birth to a second son, named Eoin. He was a beautiful, little blond-haired boy with thick curls. He reminded her so much of Tommy and whilst he did not stop her heart from bleeding for Tommy, he certainly eased the pain. *"He was a beautiful gift, sent from God,"* Nelly said, with a gentle, happy nature. He was her reason for getting up in the morning and her dreams for a better life for him consumed her day – life was good.

No one could believe the change little Eoin brought out in Hugh. To give him his due, he was very fond and proud of his little son. Indeed people were actually heard to say he had softened. He brought the little lad everywhere with him, so that he could show him off to the neighbours and strangers alike. He chatted to the boy about which cattle he would be bringing to the fair or what sheep he intended to

29

sell. It would be fair to say Nelly was very contented with life. It hadn't turned out too bad, she smiled to herself.

One evening when Eoin was about three and a half years old, Hugh said he would take care of him and brought him out with him, doing the chores. There was a station mass in the next door neighbours'; Nelly was helping out with tidying up and had a currant cake freshly baked from the morning. So with Hugh and Eoin out of the house, she went about her neighbourly duty which was usually good fun with everyone laughing together; when all was finished and dusted, they usually had a nip of the Priest's Bottle.

Hugh was busy milking away in the cow byre with little Eoin playing and scampering away with a ball outside the doorway. A barrel of water stood under the down pipe catching rain water at the side of the cow byre and Eoin threw his ball into the barrel. Not wanting to disturb his father, as he was a little afraid of the big cows, he stood on an upturned bucket. Reaching into catch his ball, little Eoin fell headlong into the barrel, his cries for help drowned by the gush and rush of milk into the aluminium bucket.

Little Eoin was beyond any help from this world when he was found. The auld tyrant blamed everyone but himself, blaming his godfather for giving him the ball, blaming his mother for going to help prepare for the mass next door. It was the nearest thing to love he had ever experienced, this child of his. He built a prominent red stone wall around the grave of the little lad. From that day on, the tyrant seemed to lose any shred of decency he had, going round the fields screaming at the cattle as if they understood and blaming the world for his problems. You would never have called him a nice man, but from that day onwards, he turned into a wicked monster, a hatred-filled man with beasts reigning in his brain and his heart.

Fostering the Boy

Michael John's friend and confidant, Tommy Lee was born to Nelly in the mid-fifties, being placed under the name of Edward Lee in the convent in Co Clare, that was ran by the Sisters of Mercy. Nelly had called him after her own father Tommy Eddie Lee. When he was two months old, the orphanage part of the convent where he resided was closed down, and the little orphans had to be placed around in different places, with the Poor Clare sisters taking in Tommy and two other little children. Now as chance would have it, Tommy had fallen on his feet and was lucky to have been moved to this orphanage – if moving to any orphanage could be considered lucky, then, Tommy's luck was in.

Unknown to anyone for quite some time, Tommy's real aunt Sr Joseph was a nun there; Kathleen, as she was known before she joined the convent, had joined the order in 1931, much to the heartbreak of her parents. This was a strict enclosed order; there was no visiting to her parents, and it had been almost like a death. One of Sr Joseph's duties was in the administration side of the adoption process, filling forms and keeping all documentation safe for the authorities; this is how she discovered Tommy's identity.

This was how she came into constant contact with Tommy, when he was sick and went out of her way to see he was not neglected. She was especially nice to him on visiting days when other children had visitors or friends' days, as Tommy had no visitors and she would surprise him with little gifts and treats the good town folk had left at the convent door. No one could understand how Tommy went to his room on these days with a smile on his face, but he could not wait to see what little treat would be awaiting him. He used to dream he had his own fairy godmother.

She also felt she was blessed by God to be able to act as guardian angel to her little nephew, Tommy. She added a special prayer of thankfulness to be able to see her nephew grow, and he was the image of her own younger brother, Bernard. As the years rolled by, he grew into a fine boy and soaked up all knowledge. She dreamed and hoped that maybe he would enter the church when he grew up, as quite a lot of the more intelligent boys entered the priesthood. She had not counted on him being a real boy, and a mischievous one at that.

When he was an altar boy, his friend Rollo had dared him to drink the altar wine. Between giggling and pushing each other around, there was as much spilt as drank, but Reverend Mother decided he was of an age where he could start to be a handful. After a lot of consideration, it was decided to foster him out, as nobody wanted children above the age of two or three. All Sr Joseph's entreaties were in vain. It really put a strain on her vocation but she confessed to Reverend Mother, and apologised, truly believing that she had been privileged to have been part of his life this far. Kissing the Reverend Mother's ring, she returned to her normal life in the convent, asking only to be spared attending the actual fostering meeting and was granted her wish.

The following Monday morning, a couple arrived with a view to fostering a young boy. The most unlikely looking couple arrived. The man looked like a poor scrap of humanity; his features were no better: he was a large block of a man, had a flat face with elephant eyes, only a stick of a nose showing and a bald shiny head speckled with brown spots like blackbirds eggs. He had this thick neck that looked as if his head had been stuck on his shoulders; his legs were short considering the length of his body, and he was bandy legged. He also sported a track of zigzag blue and scarlet veins across the face. There were better looking Bogie men pictures used to threaten children to behave and to get them to go to bed.

The woman was a contradiction in total; very pretty with pale skin and a very frail gentle disposition, and her eyes lit up on seeing the lad. She talked quietly and Tommy answered shyly. The replacement nun just could not understand; she remarked to herself that they were so familiar with one another, it was almost as if they had met before. They even looked alike, thought the nun; maybe she was being fanciful as she had been very fond of Tommy too. The tyrant decided there and then to take him home as he looked strong he thought, he could make good use out of him. So motioning to sign the papers, turning around to both his wife and Tommy, he shouted gruffly, *"Come on I have not got all day."* Going outside he flopped into the front of the hackney car and they were all driven home.

The Recognition

For the first few months, the tyrant worked Tommy hard enough, but he was quite civil to him. Nelly of course doted on him, making clothes and knitted jumpers and socks, also making a suit from material she had bought from the turkey money. She had even made a lovely shirt. She had bought him a tin whistle and a football for Christmas. Though she would have to warn him it was between himself and Michael John Finn to play with, they were great schoolmates. If the tyrant thought it was for Tommy alone, he would destroy it. Nelly sometimes felt guilty that it had been too easy replacing her own children, as Tommy and Edward would have been the same age. She often thought of Edward and Eoin; she was glad to have Tommy to shower with all the love and affection she had given both her sons. She always thought of Tommy as her third son and loved him like he was her own. He was the light of her life.

Young Tommy had been living in his new residence for about six months when the tyrant made the grim discovery. It was grim, as far as Tommy was concerned. It was a spring evening; they had both been out turning over the heap of potatoes, to prevent new growth from coming out through the clay on the side of the heap. The moon was peeping out from behind the eastern side of the mountain when they had finished. Young Tommy was tired and thirsty, so the minute he entered the kitchen, he went straight over to the black and tan earthy crock pot on the table and filled his mug full of spring water.

Sitting down at the table, his left hand rested on the table, the other dangled over the back of the chair, the tyrant shouted, *"Look at the cut of those hands, and you went and dipped into the spring water with them."* As he looked at the dirty hands closely, he left out a strangled scream. Up to now, the tyrant had displayed a certain black affection for the boy. Once, he allowed him to bring a stray white kitten home on one condition: it did not come into the house. Little Tommy had been deliriously happy, it was the first time he had owned anything live in his life, but now, he was staring at it, as if his eyes were deceiving him. With bulging eyes, he grabbed Tommy's left hand, and incandescent with rage, he whacked the tin mug he held in his own hand, like a man possessed on the little dirty hand.

Calling him a bastard, then swaying and raving away, eyes rolling around in his head, saliva dribbling from the corners of his mouth, Tommy crying silently holding his hand. Nelly, wondering what had caused his outrage and looking down at his poor little hand, noted for the first time that his clay covered index finger was joined to the next and the upper part was crooked just like the tyrant's, his father's and the three brothers' that had emigrated to America in the thirties. It had been a standing joke in the Drury's – the left-handed brigade.

Nelly swayed, blood thudding in her ears, putting her hands to her head, trying to understand. *'It can't be,'* she thought, but the facts added up, the age and birth date they gave us all corresponds. He was the same age as her own boy. There had been some mention, if he was a healthy child, that there would be rich Americans looking for babies. The nuns had gone onto tell her it was a great chance for any child; they would never want for anything. But her little boy Edward had been a very healthy baby, and had been left in an orphanage down south. Her brain went round in circles. *'It's impossible,'* she thought, *'but why could she never explain the intense protection she had felt towards the child, from first glimpse of him in convent corridor,'* she thought. She prayed fervently that Hugh would say yes. Though, all he was looking for was his bone structure, as if he was judging a beast. All he cared was that he would lift heavy weights, as Hugh had hurt his back showing off in Regan's local pub. The bet had been to lift a half-barrel of Guinness with one hand, and leave it up on the high counter. He managed to do it alright but with considerable damage to himself. His back gave in, causing him extraordinary pain. He'd tried every quack in the country, but to no avail. Doctor upon doctor, with all kinds of letters after their names, had tried, but he was still left in pain.

'Didn't I always,' Nelly thought, 'somewhere in my mind really know, or did I just not want to believe what my heart was telling me.' My god, Hugh put up with Tommy or rather he just about put up with him, before not knowing his parentage. He had been a good lad, always trying to please and had been a great worker. 'Oh, now he will make it unbearable for the child,' she thought. 'I will have to be very careful not to show any favouritism to Tommy, while the tyrant is about.' How was she going to protect him? She would have to try and please Hugh, cook all the things he liked, bake his favourite cake, not that he ever said so, just the way he liked to eat it. 'It may seem a thankless job, but anything to keep his temper away from little Tommy,' she thought. 'That, in it, would be thanks enough. The ploughing would be starting soon,' she thought, 'he would not be able to manage without Tommy's help.' Maybe with God's grace he would calm down; it was not as if anyone else knew or even guessed that he was really his son. Nelly sighed to herself why could he not be proud instead of being this way. It was not as if he did not know how Tommy had come into being.

The following morning, there was little or no change; the tyrant's hatred of most of the people in his world was always intense. Even as a youngster, Joe Kielty told us how no one could understand him. His parents had been such grand people and both brothers as well. There were tears upon tears when those boys left these native shore; emigration was a must for survival in those days. No one knew why Hugh was such an evil creature – he just loved hurting people. The first thing Nelly thought of next morning, when she got dressed, was getting a lock for the inside of Tommy's bedroom door. She'd do it today, because she got no wink of sleep the night before, fearing for Tommy's safety. Though the wind was driving sheets of rain, she walked the four miles to town, but not before she had risen at six o'clock to get the cows milked, the milk strained and cooled. She also got timber and sticks at the ready, dug the potatoes, pulled the vegetables and got all prepared. She measured the time, so she would have returned in time to have the fire down, dinner cooked and ready on the dot of one o'clock, even if she was not lucky enough to catch a lift on a turf cart or the milk cart.

The tyrant never seemed to notice nor care whether she was there or not, so long as the meals were ready. The way he knew the time to the minute was unbelievable, from the grandfather's pocket watch he kept on a gold chain in his waistcoat pocket. Five minutes before mealtimes he came home, washed his hands in a tin basin of water with a big bar of sunlight soap left on a big stone outside the back door, then he dried his hands in the flour bag towel left on the boxwood hedge summer or winter.

Now if the dinner was not on time, he would wash his hands, then go in and dry them on the kitchen curtains – he was a bad egg surely. He would sit at the table with his arms thrown around where his dinner or meal should be, holding a fork in one hand and knife in the other, as if he had his dinner, as if he was afraid someone was going to grab it off him. Just watching him, a person would be forgiven for wondering how a mean ugly specimen of a man could have fathered such a good and gentle son as Tommy.

He had received his dinner on schedule but the minute he had drank down the last dregs of his tea, he made his way up the garden and over the sty without barking any chores to Tommy, without acknowledging him at all. The remembrance quickened her blood – she held her hand jammed into her breast – it was the child's birthday tomorrow, and he had taken himself off to the little gate, to the entrance into the little red-walled grave. He would always grunt, *"I am off to see the child."* He could never say Eoin's name since he died. He never referred to him as dead, always referring to him as the child, when he went away. When going to visit the grave, he spoke as if he was going visiting him, as if he was still alive. It was the only time he showed any nature; maybe if the child had lived, he would have softened a bit, but no one will ever know now, she thought to herself. She thought maybe he would have accepted Tommy in a way if Eoin had lived, but would Tommy have ever came to live with them then?

Nelly went about fixing the lock upon the inside of Tommy's bedroom door, feeling that it would make her feel better and maybe she would get some sleep this night. She finished her chores getting Tommy to help her with the mangels to feed the cows and to give mash to the pigs. She had a great name as a pig feeder, and she used to joke it was her only claim to fame. When the tyrant returned that day, both were shivering in fear. All Hugh said was, *"Do you know where the pick is,"* and asked Tommy to find it. When Tommy returned with it, he made him accompany him saying, *"I think I will plant a few scots pine down there where the tinkers do camp in the winter. If we get the holes made and manure in them, then I can buy some young saplings at the fair in the town tomorrow and sure you can plant them in the evening."* Out they went and worked at the preparations; on returning to the house, the tyrant was back in his foul humour but strangely enough, Nelly was more at ease when he was in his usual humour than the other way. He had really scared Nelly and she had thought Tommy was in mortal danger.

Things carried on more or less the same as always with no reference to Tommy's hand ever mentioned again. It was like it had never happened. Nelly thought it was the lull before the storm and although Hugh never mentioned it again, Nelly was always vigilant. As Tommy grew in years, Nelly often caught Hugh looking with a vile glint in his eye when he thought no one was looking. Nelly often thought to herself it was probably a good job she cannot see in to the black tunnels of his mind. She could not bear to think of the black thoughts and deeds that went on in there and if he was comparing him to Eoin.

Just once she had plucked up the courage to speak to him about the likeness of the two boys, but he had growled and snarled at her saying, *"Foolish crazy woman! Never mention my son's name and that bastard in one breath ever again if you want to continue to breathe air yourself."* 'My God,' she thought, *'it was you who brought that child into the world too, it was you that raped me. He is the very same blood and genes as little Eoin; what kind of animal are you to blame an innocent for your sins. Would one not be grateful to know your flesh and blood was under the same roof as you, especially when you are getting older and more decrepit by the day?'* Shaking her head, she thought, *'Even after all these years, I still don't really know you or what goes on in your black, septic brain.'* If there was such a thing as changelings, then he definitely was one of them.

The School Days

Tommy and Michael John were inseparable from the first day Tommy entered Derrynasigh School and sat in with the third class. It consisted of eight girls and three boys, so the boys were delighted with the extra manpower. Tommy was soon up to scratch with the goings on in the school – both good and bad. Taking the teachers stick and hiding it under a loose floor board was a great favourite to reversing the time on the clock. Poor Mrs Brigid Toolan was an old lady whose husband drove her the six miles to school each day, so if the clock went back, she had to sit and wait till he came back for her thoughtless boys. Peeping over the girl's toilet wall was another big no-no. Everyone's favourite: how to take the longest way to the well to fetch water for teachers' tea, and how to trip down the steps to make it look like an accident, so off again to the well. It was such a lazy happy adventure, going according to the seasons; wild strawberries, vetches red, white and red currant, gooseberries, crabapples sour – ducks to all their own seasons. Chatting with passing neighbours and the fun times spent trying to catch frogspawn in the stream passing the school gamble. Teacher usually sent two pupils on this mission.

Tommy's world in the convent had all been routine, from getting up in the morning till going to bed at night, every week followed in the same vein, weeks running into years. He had never seen the moon, apart from through a window. Since he came to live there and got to know Michael John, his life had become one adventure after another, each season brought new things to see and do. Spring started with marbles, on your hunkers, potting your

40

thaw towards a whole in the clay. The fun of winning and swapping your best ones for a more valuable one, then going home with your bulging pockets.

Searching the bird's nests, his favourite sound of the curlew, a large brown bird with long curved bill, wading along the river when he went to collect cows, with the mound, sloping to the river, where the curlew nested. Tommy always found the nest well, just a large hollow in the grasses but the eggs were magnificent olive green with brown patches – sort of pear shaped.

It was the first spring he found the nest and of course Michael John was the only one to know the secret. Later, Mary Agnes became their confidant and true friend even though she was a girl. Another of Michael John's brain waves was to get everybody in the school to gather sugar string to make a kite. String was very scarce in the years after the war. There was uproar in the neighbourhood when kitchen drawers were found void of string. String was used for holding up trousers or replacing buttons or tag on an overcoat.

Mary Agnes Grady was to make the triangle with Tommy and Michael John. She being the only girl that never told tales on the two of them – always said she was not sure, or never knew. They always trusted her. The three of them always sat on the one bench at school, helping each other out with homework. They also loved her father; he was a character and a half, and he spent a lot of time advising easy ways of getting sums done quickly, having fun and showing them tricks with string because they were his daughter's friends.

Sometimes he despaired of his tomboy daughter, but he could not help but see how they took care of her. They resembled a family. He had lost his wife Maggie when Mary Agnes was only three to consumption. Although Jamie Grady was heartbroken, he tried to make Mary and her brother Tom, who was ten, a happy childhood. God having given him a good sense of humour helped him through. He was a great worker and handy, he was a jack of all trades, but a master of quite a few; there seemed to be no job he could not do. He paid a neighbour good money to help look after his two children. Everyone had a great admiration for Jamie.

For the man that left school at nine and a bit, his father needed his help at home to take care of the family; two wee brothers and a sister, all under six. His mother was in the old workhouse with the consumption. Jamie Grady ran the three and a half miles into the workhouse in his bare feet, with a bottle of fresh mild each evening for his sick mother, and he had to run the same road back again to let his father get out, and he would take care of his siblings. He did this run summer and winter, every evening, till his mother passed away.

His motto in life was to smile through adversity, and aim for children to have as happy a childhood as possible, which he did, along with giving time to Tommy and Mickey Agnes became sweethearts much to Michael John delight and old Jamie said, *"Well I knew that long ago,"* and smiling, he walked away.

The Meitheal

Tommy hated the rustling noise of scurrying rats and mice as they ran away from the butt of the stack of oats. It reminded him of the convent where he could hear them overhead when trying to sleep. Sometimes this rustling noise and the odd squeak now and then could be heard, and Tommy had only realised this was the nuns' habits and their shoes as they walked the corridors at night when he was much older. The nuns were always praying at all hours of the day and night.

The fear, however irrational, was already deep seated and it made him squeamish. He couldn't let his fear show as the seven lads with him were all his own age, holding shovels and spades in their hands ready to catch the escaping rats and mice. He knew he would get an awful slagging if they noticed, even though he was the only one amongst them who would go into Sheridan's bull field, teasing the bull with a red jumper. When he charged, he could clear the boxwood hedge, gorse or whitethorn with a swift leap.

Threshing always gave edge to his appetite, he thought, as he wiped the sweat from his face and expelled some air which lifted the damp curls from his brow. *'Surely it must be time for the break,'* he thought. As the older men handed the sheaves up the line to old Ballantine standing on top of the thresher, somebody mentioned old Hugh. *"Well,"* said Tommy, picking the shovel with the sharpest head, crashing down on an escaping rat, *"if only that was the tyrant's skull, the world around would be a wonderful place."*

"Poor Nelly," he said. He always felt a knot of pain when he thought of how he treated her, thinking at least she

would have some ease if he was gone. Some of the neighbours did not blame the tyrant at all. Shure did not half the men in the parish and right into the next parish ask for her hand in marriage, and she had refused them all even if it was graceful and polite and then she turns around and marries a man that was ugly in mind and body, but he had a few pounds and maybe she liked money best. Some women are like that; the fellows she had scorned reproached. Why else would she marry a man like Hugh Drury?

The threshing was going on behind Anderson's haggard and there were great sounds of merriment and craic. Someone asked Tom Ballantine was he bringing Sissy to the Wake Dance tonight. *"Oh no, she has her sights set on 'posher' than me, did you not know she has taken a shine to the new dentist in town."*

"That's right," said Tommy, "sure hasn't she had two teeth out already and says she is going back on Wednesday. *She has a right fancy on him, how will he ever shake her off. She will probably get all her teeth removed before she sees the light."* Someone heard the lid of a creamery can clash down. *"I hope poor Sissy did not hear me!"* said Tommy.

Unfortunately for Tommy, Sissy came running towards them with a jug of milk in her hand and her green eyes sparkling in her head. She called Tommy some choice names, seldom heard from the mouth of a woman, and everyone else averted their eyes, suddenly becoming very interested in the jug like they had never seen one before in their lives. *"You are nothing but a rag of a man, you will get yours if I have anything to do with it Tommy Lee or whoever you are bad zest to ya."* Oops, it would seem his luck with the fairer sex doesn't hold much weight.

"Good job for me, Mary Agnes can put up with my wicked ways," Tommy said laughing it off. When Sissy had stomped off back to the house, Charlie got ribbed about his girl Tina Tiny Weenie till Charlie lost the rag and ran after Tom Ballantine brandishing a shovel. Old Ballantine called order and they all returned sheepishly to the job in hand.

As Tommy went back to his work, Jimmy Joe Kielty said quietly to him, *"Tommy I know, gossoon, you have a lot to put up with, more than any human being has to put up with, but it is a dangerous thing to wish someone dead, I mean dangerous for you Tommy."*

"I know Jimmy Joe," Tommy answered, *"but I worry so much about Mother, especially at present. You will always keep an eye on her for me won't you if I am not there?"*

"Of course I will," he replied. Looking at Tommy, he noted there was something different about him, he had grown up into a fine young man, more confident looking forward to the future. That worn down look was gone. He had always been a good-natured lad but coming from that place where hatred lived every day, he thought about what Tommy had said, being frightened for his mother; now this bothered Jimmy Joe greatly.

He knew he always gave Hugh the benefit of the doubt being his only friend in the world since childhood lads and his first cousin. He knew his history and it did not make good reading – very sad indeed. Still not a good enough excuse for his atmospherics. Just then, Sissy returned looking like a giant caterpillar in an emerald green cardigan calling everyone into dinner. Mrs Ballantine shouted, *"Please hurry in boys before the soup goes cold."* Marie and Helen were helping their mother cook the dinner for the Meitheal. Sissy was only there as decoration, swanning around the boys, she believed they all fancied her.

The fellows all went in to eat after washing their hands in a tin basin and drying them on an auld flour bag. Taking their seats, the craic was good and the smell of the dinner was great. Mrs Ballantine was a great cook, always winning prizes for her baking and breads. The smell of whitewash was very strong; everything sparkled and the window sills and half door painted with red lead paint gleamed. The chimney too all the way up and around the cubby hole, where the bacon was smoked, had been painted.

All the preparations were made for the party to be held there that night. The good room was locked as it held all the baking, including seven rich fruit cakes and dozens of little tartlets as well as gallons of lemonade and seven gallons of dandelion wine. Mrs Ballantine had a thing about the number seven. There was half a ham all sliced into perfect slices and seven chickens all roasted and sliced. Keeping busy was the best way to keep loneliness away and to stop thinking of when all would be gone to town to see the emigrants off; the mother was usually left at home.

This time, Mrs Ballantine was changing the rules. She was going to go the whole way down to Cobh and when she waved goodbye to her first born, she was going to stay with a friend, Lizzy, in Cork City. Lizzy had a little bakery shop, and she would be staying there for a week to ease the heartbreak. At least he was going to her brother in New Jersey. The boys would be parting when they got to America which was a pity, but they will surely meet up at a football match, probably when Roscommon was playing New York. The post was much better these days too if you sent it by first mail, young Tommy had told her. *'Thank god they had all got a good education,'* she thought, *'they will be well able to write home.'*

The American Wake

Joe Ballantine and his brother John, nicknamed Tiny, because of his huge stature and big nature. Tiny's parents, sisters, brothers and friends decided to give them all a great send off, and it was a great spread in their honour. There was a goose and half side of ham cooked, two large lovely rich Christmas cakes, bread scones and small buns, sweet cakes and loads of tea bracks were on the menu. They had two large platters of butter and several people brought more bread to make sandwiches for the latecomers. The good room was opened up and laid out for ten sittings at a time – it was like a wedding.

They hadn't forgotten about the drinks either; there was tow half barrels of porter, with two large enamel jugs to pour it into the glass mugs, an endless stream of poteen along with dry sherry for the ladies, and a load of homemade lemonade and cordials. There was wine made from the local hedgerows and fresh buttermilk, the best cure for any thirst.

Pat 'The Fiddler' Drury spent ages tuning, applying rosin to the bow, right up to the last minute, in anticipation of a great night's entertainment. Pat had a hump on his back any camel would be proud to own, and quizzical facial features some said resembled a monkey, but Pat believed he was beautiful, and he was on the inside and that is all that mattered.

Pat's domestic arrangements were very frugal indeed; half a biscuit tin held his weekly provisions. His water supply was a tar barrel at the gable end of the house, and how he did his laundry was anyone's guess. The roof of the cottage had half fallen down on the bedroom years ago, his

47

kitchen was his total residence that he lived, washed, ate and slept in. Everything was covered in soot, the place was full of old cigarette boxes, polish tins and tea packets. He was never known to throw anything away, from one station to the next and there was a seven year span between them. Nobody could understand how Pat was always wearing a bright white shirt with a hankie in his top pocket that was always immaculately ironed. No neighbour could enter Pat's abode and come out clean; as some smart joker once said it was the only house he knew where you had to clean your feet when you came out of it. How, as he was always so well dressed? It remained one of life's mysteries – he and the fiddle polished to the last. It was a pity he could not play the fiddle despite the attention he lavished on it; oblivious to this minor detail, he insisted on scratching away on it anyway.

Now 'Flute', Big Jim Lavin was named, as he carried a flute with a white mouthpiece everywhere in his pocket. He was a completely different kettle of fish. He had a devoted wife, six daughters who adored their father, but Jim would not be caught dead with a tie on, not even a bow tie, but he could make that tin whistle hum and transport you to a different time and forget all your worries. He was always ready for a selection of jigs, hornpipes, half-sets and lancers, and was so gifted, he carried Pat along. Jim took frequent breaks to have a good drink and smoke while Pat would keep the noise going.

Sissy Anderson was in charge of the sweet cakes to make sure everyone got their share – a few old lads were mad on the sweet bread. A few of the boys got a plan together; one went to dance with Sissy, so she locked the parlour door and put the key in her pocket. While poor Sissy danced, another lad got the long-handled pitchfork and gently lifted the window up with a penny, sticking the pitch fork in. He slowly eased out three plates of sweet cakes, buns and biscuits, putting them into the middle of an opened jacket, wrapping the food up, then replaced the plates and closed the window. Off they went and had a rare old feast.

After Sissy elaborately thanked her dancing partner after finishing the dancing and returned to the room to do her duties, the screams she let out were like that of a banshee. Everyone was shouting for cake, asking was she eating them all herself on the sly; Sissy, needless to say, was fuming.

The craic and the feasting were in full swing at seven 'o clock in the evening, and two more musicians arrived from the half parish and all kinds of jollification ensued. Myself and a few of the lads climbed up the steps of the granary, walked over the roof of the cow house and opened the hatch door that lead into the kitchen, we sat down and let our legs hang down into the kitchen. Talk about a bird's eye views of the entire goings on. Sissy Anderson was dancing with Johnnie Ballantine. She stopped and said, *"You know I would marry ya myself, Johnnie, if you don't go to America."*

"Oh thank you, Sissy," he replied, winking up at us as if to say, well that sure is one good reason for emigration, and that would be putting it kindly.

She just smiled and said, *"You're lucky I am here at all. I was to bring Granny down to Enniscrone for a fortnight; her rheumatism is playing up. You know how she loves taking the waters every year, and I do too, but I really love the Ceili's at night, the Sligo fellas are gorgeous. So I asked Dad if we could lose one day just to say goodbye to you all, I knew you would be disappointed if I didn't."* Her father Sonny was a lovely cheerful, helpful neighbour, everyone held him in great esteem and respect, but his only daughter was the bane of his life.

An only child, Sissy's mother had died when she was three years old, and it was him and his old mother whom had reared her, but she had always been a handful. Whether she knew the difference between right and wrong was left to be debated, but she sure seemed to end up in a lot of scrapes. The last escapade back in May had taken a lot out of poor Sonny. Sissy had gone round all the neighbours' fields wearing a hood, plaiting all the cows' tails with rushes

49

saying she was putting a curse on the cows. A few months later, when all the neighbours were leaving their creamery cans at the cross by Anderson's door, which was shaded by a big tree whose shady boughs kept the cans cool in the mid-day sun – just as well, as Tom Kane, the creamery man, was never too early on the job – Sissy had started taking the cream off the top of the cans and when the creamery cheques arrived at the end of the month, Sonny got a mighty high price per gallon, his butter fat levels were sky high and everyone else that left their cans there were much lower than usual. No one could understand this; they speculated that the new field Sonny had rented near the lake must be very rich, others thought that maybe Sissy did have the power to put a curse on their cows.

This went on for a few months until a passer-by one morning noticed that the cans were wet on the outside. Next day this same young fella decided to keep watch and before his very eyes, as the last can had been dropped down for collection, Sissy appeared and skimmed the top off the milk cans adding it to their own. Caught red handed, she could do nothing, no one would have decked it, even with all the bragging about the rich milk she had made. She said no one would believe him, especially as that Tommy Lee was anything but a Maggie's boy. It was a pity she said that it was not him that was emigrating, no place in the world would be far enough away. She wished he would go to Timbuktu and the fellow that would work with him could be no better. Because of the high esteem that they held for Sonny Anderson, a new place was found, further down the road from Sissy's reach.

At 2am, the lamenting started with all the stories of the emigrants-to-be, about their childhood and all the good deeds and mischief they had ever got into in their time. The most mischievous time being the time old Flannery, a local drunk, got them all into big trouble and told oceans of tales on them. They never knew where he was, they never knew it seemed he laid down when even he got drunk, and then

50

listened behind ditches unknown to the boys. Well one night, old Flannery was coming home maggoty, well under the weather, when the boys came across him. They took the reins off the cart and brought him home. Then they took the wheels off the cart and carried the cart into the kitchen, put the wheels back on the cart, put him back in the cart and left. When he awoke the next morning, he got a big surprise; funnily enough, the boys must have turned over a new leaf, for no more tales were heard of their exploits again. Stories after stories followed about their childhood escapades, people became sadder as the morning went on, the Ballantine boy's Mother sang a few songs 'Goodbye Johnnie Dear' and 'A Mother's Loves a Blessing'. Watching Michael John, she said she would sing the 'Boys of the County Mayo' and hoped they would always be friends.

The moon had paled and the morning sky had reddened from the rising of the new day when the music ceased. From then on, it was mostly drinking that was done, you could hear a bout of crying rising from one corner or another. Michael John took his leave about five-thirty, saying he wanted a bit of shut-eye with all the driving he had. *"I'll be back at nine,"* he shouted saluting the air. At nine, he did return and all the final goodbyes started. It was a sad hour; all the men were going as far as the town with the lads, but his poor mother ran down the long garden after she said her goodbye to her boys and waved them out of the sight. His sisters stood and watched her go, as they knew she had an altar to Our Lady with flowers and candles there, where she went for solace when things got too much ever since their sister Emma had died from eating too many sour green apples.

It was some kind of poison the doctor said that caused her death. The river that ran at the bottom of the garden was the only thing that parted Mrs Ballantine and her departed daughter, lying in the little country graveyard. So the girls turned saying, *"There is no point sniffing; come on, let's clean up the place inside and out, and prepare the boys last*

Irish Breakfast. When we tidy up, we will go down for Mother and tell her she will never get rid of us. Either it will cheer her up or put her into an even greater depression." They smiled. Maura was doing a strong line with the only son of the next door neighbours and everyone was very pleased about the match. Both their fathers had been born a week apart, started school together, made their first holy and confirmation together. They had married the same summer and joked they would die the same winter, but not for a long time yet, they used to jibe. It was not unknown for the two of them to disappear for a couple of days at a time, playing cards and drinking poteen and no one batted an eye, for they were greatly loved as family men.

Looking for the Fare for America

Throwing his tag on the back of his chair, he said, *"I wish I could find the fare, Mother. I promise I would send for you within the year. They say there is great money to be made for those who are not afraid of work. Joe's cousins in America are building contractors and he is sorting all the lads out with jobs. I would love to see you live a little, Mother, and to get away from that tyrant. I would take great care of you, Mother."*

The tears glistening in her eyes, she said *"Come with me,"* going out to the dairy which was next door to the cow house. She picked up the large knife that was left there for chopping mangels that were too large for the mangler. She removed the butter and cream off the table, over to the top of the butter box. Getting up on the form, she began to remove the white-wash, working the edge of the knife around a stone. Gently easing the plaster out, she then pulled out a large flat stone. She poked behind it and pulled out a leather pouch and a walnut-plug tobacco tin. Then she said, *"Go out and check again."*

Out Tommy went, casting an eye down the road to the gate. *"No sign,"* he said coming back in quickly, eager to see what was in the tin. Well the sight nearly left his eyes, seen the leather bag now, lying empty on the table with about sixty or seventy gold sovereigns shining back at him. Then Mother pulled out three hundred pounds in red twenty-pound notes. *"How much do you need?"* she smiled.

"The fare is sixty-five pound," he said shakily. She handed him over the ten red twenty-pound notes, and put ten

gold sovereigns into the leather bag, putting the rest back into the tobacco tin with the last one hundred pounds. She replaced it back in the wall making sure to clean all traces of lime with a cloth.

Going back into the house, she handed Tommy a clean jam-jar saying, *"Go and hide this away safely till you need it."*

He put the money and sovereigns in the jar, placing them upon the table, and picked her up shouting, *"Mother, you are an angel, why don't you come with me."*

"No, Tommy, you get away, he would never doubt I helped you, and he would be so delighted to see me miserable without you, he won't bother tormenting me. I will arrange to go to meet you when Bernard comes home. He will organise everything for me. You see, it was him that placed that money in the wall for me a lot of years ago. He always pretended he was the tyrant's friend, practically ignoring me, bringing him presents and doing some of his trade work. You see, he was a coach maker; he worked for a Lord in the south of England and had a great reputation. The Lord only got him to do specialised jobs; he was very kind to Bernard and made him a wealthy man. Bernard could come and go as he pleased and would come home often to source timber for a particular job. He would always bring Hugh a present or do a bit of work around the place that needed doing.

"It was him that made the cubby hole and plastered the wall. The money he hid was in case things got impossible for me, it was a gift knowing I was not really stuck. Keeping in with the tyrant meant he could come back and forth and see me, he would leave notes sometimes, big long letters; we had a hiding place down on the shore, and I would collect them when I went for the cows, it was a great way of keeping in contact with my mother. Of course I would see her at Mass on a Sunday, but got little chance of conversation. I really loved the spring time coming around and with it the mission. I loved that week, being able to see Mother and talk to her

twice in the one day during the women's week of the missions, with Hugh safe at home as the men had their own mission week. How I used to long for that week every year to come around.

"There was another chance to escape when Hugh would go cutting turf with Mick Brennan on the cart. It was about nine miles away and they would be gone all day. This was the only time I got to see my sister Lily and her husband. When all the jobs were done, I raced down home in my wellingtons, changing into my shoes behind the ditch and rambled for nearly two hours. I could see the new line road they took and would race back up the hill before they got around the roadway.

"My life changed for the better too, when you came to live with us and being able to keep in contact with home. Now it is time you had a life of your own, do you know, I think I will be happy knowing you are away from this hatred and living a life of your own. I will dream of the day we meet again and we can be together it will fly and sure won't it take you time to get organised and find a place for us to live."

Tommy grabbed his mother and swung her around in the air, giving her a big kiss; he put her back on her feet gently once more and said, *"I better go and find a very good hiding place, probably under the gooseberry bush I was digging around yesterday, and then we will talk more before he comes home."* Off he went to find a spade to bury it safe and handy for himself. He could not believe Mother had all that money stashed away, he wished she was coming with him, he didn't like leaving her after him, but as she said, he would not bully her half as much now if he was gone.

Nelly went about her business of cutting up soda bread and taking a ham shank out of the sieve where she had left it cooling. She hummed as she went about her task; *'Thank God he would be free soon,'* she thought, and out of this house that breathed hatred every day he lived here.

Tommy returned in with a different step to him than before and pulled up to the table to eat his supper. His mother said, *"Tommy, you will have to get some clothes or maybe you could buy them on your way; I think maybe that would be safer. You must leave in the morning with Joe and Tiny Ballantine, as the American wake will go on until it is time to leave in Michael John's father's car. You can always pretend you are taking a lift into town for blue stone, for spraying as it will be the last time this year. Tomorrow is the day Mick Malarkey said it would be in stock. You are supposed to be bringing my bike home from the repair shop. I will say goodbye the night before."*

Just then they heard the creak of the gate and the dog growled. *"Mother, I'll go tell Michael John he will have another comrade. He will be delighted I am tagging along and will be happy to keep my secret along with all the others I have told him. I cannot wait to see his face. Good night, Mother, and God bless."*

The Blackest Day

The morning was squally and rough, the wind had been gathering all night. The thatch on the roof was standing on end at the eaves. The cow byre roof was screeching and rattling away under the bull wire holding the corrugated iron down. Nelly watched and listened, not hearing the wind; the noise she heard was in her soul. Seventeen years she had him close to her; *'I know I am lucky,'* she thought to herself. She had not thought she was lucky the night he came into the world, when her heart thought it would burst, and no one to share her joy with. Now he was leaving her again, although she did believe him when he said he would send for her with all the arrangements made; still, she felt it in her bones she would never see America, she was alone again with no one to share her grief this time either.

Holding the aluminium bucket as she went to fetch some water from the well, she thought she might see old Finns' car and the hackney car passing, and maybe he would wave. Oh she knew she should have been fetching Hugh's breakfast, but today that was the least of her troubles. It was funny how she did not fear him, it was like he had lost his power over her. Returning to get a second bucket to fill, she heard a roar like a wounded animal.

The tyrant was coming out of the dairy, he never enters there. Nelly thought he must have been tired of waiting for her, and gone to get some butter; she should have remembered. Like a mad man, he roared waving her leather bag with the gold sovereigns in his arms stretched up in the air. Screeching and roaring, and calling her a slut, *"Do you think you are a cash cow?!"* Nelly could hear but couldn't see him, and they met outside the byre door. Nelly dropped the bucket and made a run for it, but he was faster and grabbing the shovel that was propped against the white-washed wall, he felled her with a wallop to the head. Blow after blow, he reigned till his rage was spent and without even looking at Nelly, he grabbed the money and headed for the old nunnery graveyard.

After a while, Nelly, bleeding and badly injured, managed to drag herself to the roadside gate. Each inch was torture, and she had no idea how long it took her; past caring if the tyrant was around or not, she began praying for some kind soul to come to her assistance before passing out. Jimmy Joe Conlon arrived with his horse and cart. He spotted her half way out on the road; feeling for a pulse, he wasn't sure if there still was one. He lifted her gently into the floor of the trap and hurriedly went to town, heading straight for the workhouse which was the nearest thing to a hospital at the time.

Her usual pale face was now ashen, it's dazzling fairness normally set off by raven black hair, now was matted with blood, it hung lank and in clumps. She spent three hours there feverishly, fingering the scapular Tommy had bought her at the last mission, whispering and praying, her last words, *"Oh Tommy why now, my son."* A mother's dying words, heard by those around her, only herself and Michael John knew he was leaving for America with the other lads. She was saying goodbye to her beloved son, her last thoughts of him, but the people thought she was saying he had done it.

Silence Is Not Always Golden

As poor Nelly had been crawling her way out to the gate, the tyrant had gone to the nunnery graveyard, ranting and raving, crashing through the tombstones like a demented man. With the super-human strength that sometimes comes from the mentally unstable, he lifted the slab up to throw the monies; he took the gold out of his pocket to throw it in the grave for safe keeping but his left hand slipped, ending up losing his grip, the slab came down on his head, his spirit, good or bad departed this world.

No one could believe a man of his age could have the strength to lift up the slab. Nor did they know he was the one who had come across Nelly thinning out the turnip patch and singing to herself. No one would know that tale from twenty years ago. Jimmy Joe Dwyer stumbled along the river bank around eleven o'clock, along with his friends Joe and Malachi from the American wake. Passing by the cut in the river, he saw Tank McHugh in the old nunnery graveyard like a raging bull, nothing new for him of course. Tank was trying to lift up an old headstone, covered in blood he was, probably had killed a pig that morning, thought Jimmy Joe. He parted with his friends outside the widow Kelly's house, telling the boys he wanted a drink of water for his hangover, and when the boys had gone on up the road, went in.

Now Jimmy Joe was no oil painting but Mary Kelly had a soft spot for him; of course he went in. Whatever transpired that evening, Jimmy Joe never came forward to say what he had seen. If Tommy had been caught, maybe he would have come forward, but for a grown man, he was still in mortal fear of his father. His father ruled the household with an iron will. Whatever he said went, and he was obeyed without question. It would not be good for his father to know he was keeping company with Widow Mary Kelly, knowing his father considered her a different class to them – whatever class that was, Jimmy wondered – but nevertheless held his peace.

Sissy Anderson on the other hand came forward with information which painted Hugh Drury a saint without wings. Her dislike of Tommy after the incident of laughing behind her back still rankled on, a woman scorned and all that. Had she not heard him say with her own ears as he smashed the shovel down on the rat's head, that: *"He wished it was Hugh."* She went on to tell the Gardaí how he had said: *"It would be a great world without him,"* and to add insult to injury, added another piece about him saying: *"He would get all the money,"* as old Mrs Drury fancied him, and everyone knew how good she was to him.

Only a few people knew he was her real son, or that she had even had a baby. Hadn't she gone to Cork for nearly a year with an aunt who had a cake shop, whom was not in the best of health and how Nelly had gone to night classes to learn how to type? No one ever doubted the truth of it, they believed she had been helping her aunt, and getting an education in return. Mrs Conroy, who had taught her, was a dear friend of her aunt's so no lies had been told, only a bit of economy with the truth. Hadn't she put it to good use on her return, writing letters for people who had no glasses, as it wasn't the done thing to say you couldn't write. Christmas was as busy a time for Nelly. Any written work that needed to be done, Nelly would do it, and indeed she would help anyone all day long.

The Nun's Graveyard

On the west side of Drury's house, an old nunnery was situated with most of the walls still remaining. It was a spot everyone with sense gave a wide berth. It was chilly and creepy, even on the hottest day in June, as it was said it was a place one would take the long road to avoid. It may have something to do with the gateway having a hawthorn surround and a giant oak tree that neither the east nor west wind could stir or shake. On the right hand side and on the left were two large ash trees on which dust had settled for over a century.

The old folk used to warn all the kids away from the 'fairy triad' and according to legend, fairies can be found there. Especially as it was situated smack between Charlie O'Gara's fairy fort and McGreevy's fairy fort rings. Also, it is in the very spot where the wee folk, or the good people, crossed Lough Gara from fort to fort on November eve. Even in the thorn bushes surrounding the burial place, if you looked close enough at those gnarled bushes, you could see the shapes of old witches in their branches. Some say this spot was associated with witchcraft and witches, of how they could transform themselves into trees. Others said, which seemingly seems more likely, was that in the sixteenth century, the British soldiers brutally murdered a priest saying mass on the rock on the shoreline, and then raping nine nuns before impaling them on the trees around the cemetery.

Whenever the wind blows from the northeast in November, wailing sounds can be heard. On dry November days, one can see a soot-like sticky substance; the story being handed down is that it is blood from the massacred nuns and priest. Even the pink cabbage rose that grew in the summertime by the headstones is a sad looking straggly thing growing from a rocky dry soil. This is the spot Tommy came to when he could not handle the foster father, as he was such a tyrant, but also a coward, he would be caught within a hundred feet of this spot.

One day, when Tommy had gone to the market in town with potatoes to sell, the white head cow broke into the grounds of the nunnery, the tyrant waited till Tommy returned, and gruffly told him to milk the cow, as she was the only cow milking at the time, as the others were near calving. So having done without milk all day, Tommy knew he was safe to take refuge there. Now Joe Kielty had once told Tommy that the tyrant would wake up in a lather of sweat, and the dream was always the same, even if he only nodded off on a chair. Joe said, "*It was told to him, long ago when they were only teenagers, about the constant nightmare – it never varied. He was lifting a headstone in the nunnery with a crow bar, and sticky red blood on his hands and then everything went black, and he always saw the three crows looking searchingly at him with their beady eyes.*"

Tommy had noticed in the evenings, especially in summer time when the crows would be cawing as they were winging their way home to roost in a cluster of trees in McGreevy's haggard, he always went quiet, no matter how mad he was, or what he had been shouting about; when they passed over, he always seemed to forget what he was saying. Even if a neighbour who would shoot a crow and hang him over the potato patch or maybe on top of a stoke of oats, he just shivered as he passed by; he seemed angry at whoever had done the shooting. Now that was something for a man that had no feeling for humans or animals.

This spot had another reason for people seeing and hearing things. Just between two rocks shaped like a cross, underneath them a container of poteen and a ladle lay, where the lads came and dropped a coin or two and drank to their hearts' content.

The poteen belonged to a man who lived up the mountain over the other side of the lake. The boys had made a shelter out of sallies and rushes, and left an old horse cart in it. Their own shebeen, with all the rationing going on, with butter, meat, sugar, tea, cheese, chocolate and sweets, there was no rationing with alcohol. No exciseman could catch him, because it was two miles from the nearest road to get there. No proof of who did own the poteen. Ireland always had too many heroes for anything good to come out of it. But this poteen maker was one they were not going to get. All along the lakeshore was covered in wild dog roses, the delicate cream colour that turns into red rosehips that were gathered in the autumn. Their uses were many.

With some, Aunt Maggie made into a cough medicine to keep us cough free through the winter; some were made into wine and kept along with dandelion wine in the dairy for visitors or any excuse for taking a drop. Looking over the ferny shoulder of the Curlew Mountains on the southern side, the dog or fox now free, running on around the corner and lost to sight. A gust of wind shivered amid bulrushes and sedge grass, musical crescendos then dying away like Beethoven's airs on a string. The wish-wash of the ripples sounded on the wet grey shingles at the shore. Just over a bit is where the trees stopped and a tigín, or a small wooden house, stood that Maggie Plunkett lived in.

Now Maggie was a woman of the roads, whom Nelly had befriended many years ago. Everyone can remember quite vividly, the depth and timbre of her voice, how it drew each person to her, rapt and fascinated into her world of storytelling. Nelly was forever trying to fix her up with a neighbour who lived along the shore a wee bit; it was not a road, only a footpath made by Jack O'Mara on his way to and from his cottage. Jack was a man of small stature, he only had the one coat and a pair of wellies turned down and a bald head, but you could not be blamed for thinking he had hair, as the people said he never had been washed since the mid-wife washed him.

Poor old fella O'Mara, they called him – mind you, they named him aptly; it was not long if you would be standing near him that you would find yourself scratching. Many a great yarn he told; you would stand in your bare feet in the snow to hear him, the way he would tell the story, you would be forgiven for thinking you yourself were there. He was sheer magic, I don't think he knew what the truth was, but we thought he was great. Some fellow once said, *"Sure you could find no one lazier man in Ireland than Jack, sure he loved work so much he would lie down beside it."* His domestic arrangements were very frugal indeed: his larder a half a biscuit tin, his water supply was a tar barrel at the gable of the house. His light, he dried out rushes with the skin taken off and after they were dried, he would dip them into a jam jar of paraffin oil and light them.

Once, asked how as he had no clock, how did he know the time to get up, *"Oh, when the fleas start biting at noon, I know it is time to get up. Sure I have the train for the rest of my timing. Then on a Sunday, don't I hear the two parish bells, I have plenty of time to get fitted up for mass."* Some say he slept in the hayshed at night because the house was haunted, but no more like the stories about the nunnery. The reasons were closer to home: he could not sleep with the fleas biting him. It was no wonder Maggie preferred the cold-wet roadside, which was before the council had built the wee house for him to share with the flock of fleas. Poor Nelly always thought maybe the love of a good woman like Maggie would get rid of them, that would straighten both Jack and the house up.

But sure there is class distinction up and down. Sure his father had left him quite comfortable with a cottage – slated – a grand thing in those days, and a piece of good land and a nice piece of bog; sure the neighbour would cut it and save it for him, so they could have a dozen yards for themselves, but Flea could not be bothered. He would rather spend the day making weird noises on the flute or the fiddle, whatever instrument he was learning that week.

Someone once said, "*You were as well stuffing money down the rat hole than to give it to Flea.*" When he did own cows, the poor things could be heard into the next parish lowing to be milked; it was a terrible thing to hear, the agony of the cows loaded down with milk. He was heard to say the cows on one hot day, as he was saving hay, "*If you want hay next year, you would save it yourself, because I will not save it,*" and he was true to his word. All the neighbours were glad indeed when he got them all sold and let the land out. Now, it was not badness on his part but pure laziness, it was with Nelly's insistence that he sold them off.

Well, the neighbour had the task of telling Flea about the death. Some had seen him come home on the train, even though no one knew where he went. But one thing was for sure, he was devastated when he heard about Nelly, as she baked him soda cake daily since his mother went to her heavenly abode ten years ago. He used to say I am going down for the bun. The murderer had a lot to answer for, poor Jack will die of the hunger, and sure there is no one near to give him a bit to eat, unless poor Maggie takes pity on him. Oh the neighbours will try and get him something for a while, but when he goes odd again, no one will notice. He wept like a child on hearing the news. It was a hard night, no one knew what to say to him. All Flea could say between sobs, "*Oh so much blood has been shed in this area, it is the devil's own place; no one will rest till someone is found for the murder.*"

65

The Double Wake

The day after the murders, the whole town-land and surrounding area was in shock. Everyone seemed to speak in whispers; actually, if one listened, you would swear even the trees, bushes and grass was whispering too. The evening of the wake was a very harsh one indeed; the wind was coming from the northeast, and it was windy, wet and very cold. Any December night would be proud of the sting in it. It felt as if the weather knew of all the happenings. Although their two earthly bodies were laid out in the old workhouses in Boyle, Joe Kielty went over and asked the Lees if they should hold a wake. They thanked him for the suggestion asking Joe to do the arranging, as they didn't feel in control of the situation at all. Well, apart from the Lees wanting to choose the coffin. When all were in agreement on the other arrangements, Joe, and another couple of neighbours, went around the neighbourhood and spread the word.

Their first grim task was to go and choose the two coffins, then they went to the priest's house to make the funeral arrangements. From there in, they all ran into trouble; not alone did the Lees want a much better grade of coffin, they actually insisted on an oak, lead-lined coffin, like a bishop's coffin, for their daughter and sister, and they also wanted to have Nelly buried with her own people. The Lees also let it known, in no uncertain terms, that they did not care if Hugh Drury was buried in a tea chest. People were beginning to think this terrible tragedy of Nelly's death was unhinging the Lees' brains. They could maybe understand, the mother, as she was going up in the years, but the brother and the sister showed the same dislike of Hugh

Drury. Nobody refers or speaks ill of the dead as the saying goes, 'no matter what kind of being he was when alive, he was sure to be a great man when he was dead'. The priest and neighbours were in shock at this, as the Lees where very gentle, easy-going people that would not and never had caused a ripple of bother to anyone or anything. Even when everyone, although they got it hard to believe, all blamed Tommy, even if they did have doubts – why did he run away? The Lees insisted to look elsewhere for they swore Tommy was innocent of such a heinous crime. They could not tell of the relationship, as that might even put a slant of more guilt on poor Tommy.

It was a sad eerie feeling going up the boheen to the house. They only sound to be heard was either animal or fowl, the squawking of a gaggle of geese that Nelly had left out on the oat stubbles to fatten up for Christmas. Poor Jip, the sheep dog, was tied out on a long rope to protect the geese from the fox. Nelly had left a tar barrel on its side with a coat inside, but his food and water bowl were empty. The hens and ducks, along with the kittens and a marmalade cat with three legs, came running down the pass to meet the women going up on their way to tidy up the house. If they could talk, they would probably have some story to tell – or at least say we are hungry.

Joe and the others went into the village and bought a few crates of double diamond, a half barrel of both full porter and a few bottles of sherry for the older ladies. In the grocery store, they bought a couple of currant bracks, a few packets of Marietta biscuits and a few hundred Gold Flake cigarettes. The women in the vicinity cleaned up the kitchen, washed the stone floor out, cleaned the windows, white washed the fire place up the chimney as far as possible and covered all the mirrors in the house with cloths. Nelly and Hugh's chairs were turned upside down on the table. On the tables and around the fire place, the women placed the cigarettes on saucers and placed them strategically all around the kitchen, also in the rooms and outside in the shed, where the stout was been pulled from the half barrels. If ever a corpse house was eerie, that house of McHugh's was it. As twilight covered the neighbourhood, people started to gather from all over – some, because it was the done thing; others, for morbid reasons, and more to find out more about what had happened.

The priest for that part of the parish was a young man called Fr O'Malloy; he came out early in the night blessing all around the house and out in the yard where one of the murders had taken place. Returning back to the house, he said the rosary. Then he sat down with a small drop of whiskey and wanted to talk about the deceased. He had not been long in the parish, but he knew Nelly well and thought very highly of her. When he asked questions about Hugh, Bernard Lee sniggered, and said, *"Who would want to know about that animal?"* Everybody looked in shock at these words coming from this man, it damned beyond belief. Never, had anyone, ever, seen this man angry, in his or her lives. He had been in England for the past twenty years, coming home twice a year to see his mother. His job did entail travelling back and forth to Ireland for different kinds of timber he liked to use in his job; it was for a wealthy man he worked for in England. The poteen flowed and Bernard drank and drank. Then he started crying into his poteen, saying he probably deserved to be murdered, *"As many a time I wanted to do it myself,"* he said, *"but not my beautiful sister; all she ever wanted in life was to follow in Mary Agnes's steps, but not for that bastard."*

"Now," everyone said, *"come on, be fair, sure she married Hugh of her own free will."*

"Sure look at all those grand lads around the countryside that would have married her as quick as looking at her, but sure it was the money she was after," said Paul Mullany. *"Sure was I not one of them myself."*

Bernard had not heard the last words as he screamed in anger, grabbing Paul by the collar of the coat; he thumped him an unmerciful blow in the mouth. All the able-bodied jumped up to help, but no one could understand; the two of them were very well liked men. Pulling them apart, they shouted to Bernard, *"God Almighty, man, we know you have been through hell, but you have no excuse to go thumping poor old Paul. Is he not only saying what everyone thought? Did not poor Paul try to do everything to stop Nelly from marrying Hugh apart from kidnapping her!"*

Bernard kept saying, *"You know nothing, nothing at all."*

"Well, can you tell us then?" some of the boys asked.

"Not while my mother is alive or until she tells me I can go ahead and tell you all. But I am telling you, you know nothing!"

Things quietened down; someone placed a cold cloth on Paul's face and Bernard grunted, *"I am so sorry, Paul, I should never have hurt you."*

"It's alright," Paul said. *"You have been through enough."* Talk went on about local things but after a while, it came back to about Tommy and everyone had their own ideas on it. Bernard said nothing, until someone came up with the notion that he must be guilty, as why else would he run away. Bernard jumped up, but as he did, so did two or three more, and they grabbed him. *"That's enough – either tell us what is eaten' ya, or we will have to lock you up till you are sober."*

There and then he burst into talk, talking quickly, the story bursting from him, and those that managed to follow him, were in such awe of all the secrets and lies that had been threaded through poor Tommy's life. There was not a dry eye in the house.

"Ah sure we knew it was not Tommy, but it was easier to think that than to think it was someone sitting here."

"My God, the poor kid, but sure he was happy enough with his mother. He was sure enough when he was younger, but as he got older, he felt he should be able to protect his mother. He was going to send for her as soon as he got lodgings and a job. Nelly had a nice bit of gold and money of her own.

"His mother had told him most things and he worked out the rest himself. Tommy had told his mother about this fairy godmother he had in the convent, and all her kindness, how he had loved to be sick, because it was then he got all the attention. Now his mother had told him of his aunt that was in that convent and her name was Mary Agnes. Just before she took her final vows, she wrote to her mother, telling her she was taking the name of Sr Joseph. How he had yelled at her, that was the nun who was always lovely to me, I really loved it there, he told his mother. He had found out from what his mother said and how religious she was, that she had wanted to join the nuns. He also had found out for himself that his mother had always blamed herself because of the rape, thinking if she had prayed hard enough, it would not have happened. She had been singing a love song, then she looked up to him and said, sure I was always humming a tune, there was always music in our house."

No one had spoken since he had started to talk, just nodding of heads, no one put as much as a glass to their lips. He told them how Tommy was to emigrate to America with Michael John and the Ballantine boys, but no one knew Tommy's story, only Michael John – he more or less knew everything. They were afraid to tell anyone in case someone let it slip. Bernard said, *"I do not know what harm I have done, telling all to you this night, but that is the truth. I am sorry, Paul, that was why she could not marry you, or any man. She did not want the truth to come out for her mother's sake, and the girls and myself."*

"It would not be right," he said, *"and I kept her wishes till now. I will go in a while, as I should not have stayed this length away from my mother, it will be the end of her. We don't know if Mary Agnes will be allowed home for the funeral or not. I want you to wake my sister the way she deserves, and do whatever you wish about him."*

After another rosary had been said, Bernard placed his cap on his head, and said, *"Good night and please God, keep us safe this night,"* and he disappeared into the darkness bound for his mother's house.

The Chase

Joe Ballantine's aunt, Lucy Harran, lived outside, well on the outskirts of Youghal, as new houses and cottages and the odd shop broke the look of the half mile. Joe's mother had written to her a week ago and arranged for Joe to stay overnight with her – instead of herself, as she was having chest pain – and she said he would have a few friends with him. Mrs Ballantine had promised to send her sister fresh country eggs and butter, and told her she was in luck with the timing of the boys going down as the killing of the pig had been taking place, just a week ago. So she would send a lump of bacon, sausages and black pudding.

She told her not to worry he had said they don't mind, any old shake down would do and they would be delighted with her taking them in for the night. Well on arriving late that night, the boys were wrecked from the night before with the lack of sleep and all the excitement, good and bad, that had occurred in the last twenty-four hours. That was not taking into account the parting was quite wrenching for the Ballantine boys, because they were real mammy's boys. Of course Michael was very sore having to take his leave of his dear aunt, and Tommy had found it extraordinarily hard worrying about leaving his mother even if it was to make improvements in her life.

The next morning, Tommy said, after a great feed of rashers, sausages, eggs and fried bread, *"I just want to trot into town, as I have a few things I want to see to before I go and purchase a few bits of clothes for the journey."*

"Old Hugh didn't actually buy me a new wardrobe along with his best wishes," he laughed; the boys smiled

72

back but only Michael John knowing the true story. Actually, the Ballantines did not even guess that old Hugh was Tommy's father, while talking between himself and Michael John. If anyone mentioned of the wrath of his father, the others just thought he meant to say foster father.

"I will be back for the taxi. We have plenty of time yet. See you boys and thank you very much, Mrs Harran, for a wonderful breakfast and letting us stay the night. Is there anything you would like to bring back for you?"

"Will you bring me half a stone of flour? I get it very hard to carry it agra, wait one second till I get my purse."

"No Mam," Tommy shouted, *"it will be my treat."* Off he went kicking pebbles, as he walked along, not a happier man in Ireland. Whistling Miss McCleod's reel on the way, he soon reached the town centre. He went to go into a stationary shop where he wanted to buy writing paper, envelopes and a small present to send back to his uncle, for he would place under the stone below at the lakeshore, so mother would have something soon to remember him by.

'Then he could send her news from America, but that would take some time,' he thought. It would be a nice surprise for his mother – that was of real importance to him. Also, he needed to look in a drapery shop to buy up a few bits he needed badly for travelling. Just then he heard a newspaper vendor shouting very loudly about a double murder in the small town of Boyle in County Roscommon, the suspect down south. Though he knew he was only down the south, yet it seemed so far away, it seemed incredible to hear such a terrible event in his own home town, where he never heard of murder in his lifetime. He was so shocked, he felt like shouting 'I am from there'. Going up to the newspaper stand, he went to buy a newspaper for himself and there in front-page news a was a photo of himself; it had been cut out of a photo of the tug of war team taken last month, when they won against Ballygran. He felt such a weakness come over him that a concerned Cork woman asked him if he was all right. *"Yes, yes,"* he replied.

"Do you still want the paper?" she asked him; he was still in shock. He handed her the money for the paper, then glided out of the shop, oblivious to the shop lady calling him back for his change. Tommy disappeared around the next corner. He was inclined to run but could not stop himself from breaking into a trot to make some distance between him and the shop, the woman's voice and the till ringing in his ears. It was then he realised that he had handed in a pound note for the paper, and that they were probably only making a fuss about that, not that they had recognised him.

Slinking back to Mrs Harran's house, he came upon a park with some seating. He sat down beside a stream that had a low flood, the water crossing over the stones was making a hoarse whisper. The words on the page were blurring with the tears that fell. *"My lovely mother,"* he cried to himself. He had always feared his father would injure her, but he had been murdered too, so it could not have been him. *"God, just when I was happily going to make a new home for mother, to give her some freedom and happiness in the end of her days, now she is gone. I am being blamed for it all, what can I do?"* he cried to himself. *"Everyone knew how much I hated him. I should go and hide, maybe try and escape, but they will be looking for me at the boat."* After debating what he would do for nearly three hours, he thought, *'This is no good, he had better get back and see if anyone can help him. Michael John will know what to do.*

As he turned the corner for Mrs Harran's house, thinking of all that happened in the few short hours since he had left that morning, he saw an ambulance with its blue light flashing outside a house. His heart was beating wildly in his chest, with his mouth hanging open; he stared incredulously as he seen that it was parked outside number six, Mrs Harran's house. This day was going from bad to worse, he thought, as two ambulance guys came out carrying a stretcher. The only thing visible was the grey hair with a soft golden sheen of the patient. Poor Mrs Harran, what was going on; this day was getting out of control. As she stood in a trance, he overheard a man behind him telling his companion that, *"Mrs Harran had visitors from Roscommon; a nephew and three of his friends had stayed overnight as they were due to sail today. One of the lads, Tommy Lee, had ventured into town shopping,"* he had said, *"but when he still hadn't returned when the taxi came, they could delay no longer. His friends had asked the taxi driver to drive around the centre of town to see if they could find him before heading for the boat.*

"Lucy Haran's friend had only found out the other fellow was wanted for murder when she read the paper her friend had brought around to show her the front page headlines. As the lads came from the town mentioned she thought they might know the murdered people. She had given Lucy a hand preparing for the lads coming, she had been hoping to get acquainted with them last night, but they had arrived too late. Lucy had collapsed after reading the paper and they had to call the ambulance."

The man and woman behind parted company and the man stared at Tommy, unnerving him. Tommy started shaking; he turned on his heels and ran. He could hear them shouting, but like a man was being chased by a pack of hounds, he kept running. Miles and hours later, Tommy was still running across drains and fields.

By now, he had reached the town land of Gurtlylea outside Youghal. The police had nearly caught up with him; he had thought he was a goner, but managed to give them the slip, crossing roads and hiding under hedges. They had chased him up this long bohreen, dogs barking madly and men shouting excitedly. A gate ahead was closed, it seemed locked, and he thought to himself, *'I suppose they will expect me to cross the gate. They will have a clean shot of me there.'* Quickly, Tommy spotted the marring fence with a big tree beside it; grabbing a hold of a large bough from the beech tree, he swung himself over four rows of barbed wire fences and landed in the shade of a whitethorn bush.

Running on, he had spotted a drain and felt he could lie low there. When he reached it, he discovered it was a dry shallow drain, and then he heard the yelp of dogs behind him. Just as his heart, as well as his spirit, was about to give way, he slipped beneath a tuft of grass. Falling, he held onto a fist full of grass; he had fallen into an underground stream that carried water from one turlough to another, flowing away to wherever the water went. Nobody seemed to know where he was. A trickle of water flowed beneath. As the light showed through, he realised if he stood up, he could look out and see around. Then sitting down, his heart began to beat semi normal. Thinking to himself as he looked around, he tried to feel the smallish rocks, piling them together, he sat down upon them and thanked God for this miracle. As these thoughts flashed through his brain, dogs were growling over his head. It was now that his heart stopped in his breast. His ears were now pounding with the rush of blood. He did not hear what was shouted from one man to another man, as he told him of the daft dog was after a rabbit down a burrow and whistled the dog away. *"He must have crossed the gate, come on,"* a voice shouted. Tommy, taking an apple out of his pocket, munched away; then laying his head on a dry narrow stretch, lay down his head. As relief flooded through him, he realised just how tired he really was. He slept fitfully for a time; when he woke, no stream or shimmer of light was to be seen. Turning, he went back to sleep again, but these were dreams of himself and Michael John, running across drains and ditches with Shep scalping at their heels, the thought of the laughter in his throat. When he awoke the next time, there was a light to be seen, then building stones together, he looked about collectively and climbed out. He then took the way towards the sea, so climbing over a mountain.

After the Escape

Tommy climbed out of the underground drain cautiously; on having a good look around, he realised it was really a wilderness. Not a house or barn to be seen. To the left about a mile as the crow flies, there looked like a large clump of beech trees clinging together; they looked as if they were hiding a house. Otherwise, it was a bleak and lonesome mountainside apart from a few very skinny black-faced sheep. Then he really stretched himself and tried to bring circulation back to his poor body. In the last twenty-four hours, he had been to hell and back, again both mentally and physically. *'It is a good job one cannot go ahead in life and flush out the ambushes,'* he thought to himself.

One thing he had discovered from his mother was his true identity; strange he had felt what he thought what it was to have a Mother since he came to live with the Drurys – he rolled the name around on his tongue – his own name by right, he thought. *'I would prefer to keep the name I have already got used to. Sure it was my mother's name anyhow,'* he thought to himself. Oh! So much going around in his head, he had promised his mother he would not think of anything she told him till he was aboard the ship.

Then it would not matter anymore, she had said, it seemed then her eyes glazed over some, and then lifting her head as she slightly shook it, she said, *"I just wanted you to know the truth. It just seems important now tell you now."*

Shaking his head, he clutched it; he said aloud to himself, *"There would be plenty of time for thinking things through if I did not get out of here safe."* Then putting his hands over his eyes, he tried to get his bearings. He could see the sun in the east, so it was west he wanted to go.

So he went half walking and half running; he felt quite safe really. Now hunger was another thing apart from an apple, nothing had past his lips since Mrs Haran's fry-up.

He tried to soak the drink up in his system. *'Well I know it is dangerous but I must try and get something to eat.'* So he edged his way towards the house; there was a winding half obliterated cart track leading up to the house, but he could see smoke rising up out of the chimney. *'I will chance getting closer; they look like apple or pear trees,'* he thought to himself. Just then, something big, black and furry came flying, knocking him off his feet. As he sat upon the ground winded, he heard a voice say, *"Come home, girl,"* then he saw the outline of a sheepdog; the man was quite near now and he looked down on Tommy as if trying to study face.

"Sorry about that, but she is a friendly old girl. I know it is no good asking did you lose your way." He kept looking, trying to judge Tommy as he was pretty well dressed for a tramp, then saying quietly, *"Are you on the run, mate?"*

Tommy blinked, and then answered, *"You could say that, I suppose."*

"Well, I will ask you one more question: 'are you from north of Cork?'"

Again Tommy nodded his head.

"Right now you can stay safely with me for a few days. It will be Wednesday night before I can get you away. There are some fishermen from around the coast, and they call for a drink in Mick Macs on that night, before they were to head on to Cobh. It is there they will get you on the large trawler that collects the catch from smaller boats. I know one fellow that will help and take you up to the north of Scotland; from there, you can get lost."

"So many Irish migrants, you can trust them."

"I have dealt with them before okay friend." That night when they had supper, it had being a soda cake baked by the bachelor himself with a thick lump of cooked bacon,

78

sprinkling drops of holy water on Tommy, after pulling out the settle bed and indicating Tommy into it. Then pulling this large chair with thick patchwork quilt, he filled two tin mugs of poteen and they started to drink. *"Tom Nolan is the name,"* the host said. *"Now I do not want to know your name but if you ever get near Glasgow, call on this man; now it is only a nickname but he will find you work on some outcrop up in the Shetlands or the like. They don't ask questions and it is there you can lie low till you think it is safe. Now, there are no papers up that far but that will suit you. In the meantime they went off next to cull some trees and are chopping it up."*

The following night they went to meet the men; all went according plan. Whilst the men went in Mickey Macs' bar for a few jars; one man remained on deck. The only bit Tommy had not been told was for the whole journey north, Tommy had to hide under a pile of fish with only a wisp of straw to keep him breathing. The skipper said he was taking no chances of being caught with a valuable cargo, as you are really never more than a mile of shore most of the way. There were quite a number of shores to ship raids taking place at regular intervals. *"Sometimes, it was not safe to trust crewmembers,"* he whispered.

Well nearly nine hours later, the skipper called Tommy to rise and shine, the other lads had gone ashore. Handing Tommy a lump of soap and a razor, he told him to go down and wash-up. On coming up, he handed Tommy some tea and a piece of pie. As they were about to say their farewells, the skipper handed him a note with an address on it, and twenty pounds in Scottish currency. Looking up to the skipper, he was about to open his mouth when the skipper winked and said, *"No, Tommy Nolan gave me money and said to change it for you, with the wish that you never get caught."* Then he saluted Tommy, it was he said 'Tiocfaidh ár la' – all fell into place.

"They thought I was an IRA man on the run, choking, I saluted back with a thudding heart and was soon gone out of sight in the mist at White Haven."

Scotland

Tommy settled in to his new life with great ease apart from being colder, seeing a lot more snow and wind than he was used to, easing his way to the customs and ways of the north-western scots. Well he liked their music, which they did a lot of in every house at evening time. He liked sheep, but he had not much knowledge about the little woolly things. This lack was soon turned around with the help of Jock. Also, they were breeders of different strains.

Soon he had learned so much about sheep husbandry. *'Funny,'* he thought, *'at home I never knew how many sheep there was.'* He thought was it not queer how these little fluffy animals could get under your skin. Now Jock Molloy, the man who had been the essence of kindness, and his wife Alison took care of him, treating him as their own. Sure had not Alison made every stitch of clothes he stood up in, from the sheep's wool and material brought home from Glasgow.

Tommy lived a kind of existence he always dreamed his mother and him could have spent together. That was the only fly in the ointment; poor Mother – how he wished some happiness and peace for her, although she never stopped referring to how wonderful it was to have him so close. *'If only one could go ahead in life and flush out the ambushes,'* Tommy thought to himself.

Just maybe if he had been satisfied with his lot, but then the minute Michael John had mentioned immigration to America, he had never known a content moment. Then those few precious days, of Mother and him sharing all the secrets – past and present – was his blessing. Mother had seemed so young those days, he had even heard her sing around the cow house if she had felt sad about his leaving, and it sure was overtaken with being able to give him his freedom. Oh maybe she really imagined herself following him, growing old with him, taking care of her. He liked thinking she was happy those last few days she spent upon this earth.

How he longed for news from around the old home place, but they were so far out, it was very isolated. Then that was the safety. It was only twice a year the Molloys went into Glasgow. The wee radio they had was near useless, they could catch some news on a fine, wind-free day, but any bit of wind or snow and the atmospherics, all you could do was switch it off.

He loved spending time fishing off the crags, and picking the seaweed off the beach. Life would be good if only he knew how his beloved Mary Agnes was doing. *'I hope she forgets me and finds someone who she can love,'* well that's what he thought from the head but got it hard to believe from the heart. She was the only girl he had ever looked at, never mind loved. They had it all planned; he had told her everything about his coming into this world, the orphanage and all about his parentage. He had asked to keep his secret and when he could, he would send for her. She had agreed with him about his mother coming to live with them in America; she agreed whole-heartedly.

Well you see, Mary Agnes always thought his mother was nothing short of a saint, and she cared deeply for her. She had insisted it would be no heartache on her. Insisted she did that; his mother would be at the centre of their plans and she meant it. Tommy often wondered why he loved Mary Agnes so much – again he wondered – sure they had the same personality, always caring about someone else, never seen to be giving into even the gentlest despair, always looking at some good in everything. Jock Molloy had at last given in to Tommy's begging to try and get in touch with Mary Agnes. At last, Tommy had convinced him she could be trusted. So they started planning how they would get someone Jock knew, to get in contact with Mary Agnes as no letter could be chanced. But like all good planning, it takes time, having to be planned down to every detail, then just when all could be put into motion, something unexpected happened. It put a full stop to any arrangements of his dreams – of contact with his beloved.

It came in the shape of a tragedy; a bombing occurred in northern England. The two Molloys suggested to Tommy that maybe it would be safer if he immigrated to Australia to a cousin of theirs, who had a large sheep station and needed help. It was nearing the shearing season, needed was especially someone good at handling sheep. If he liked, they would make all the arrangement quickly for him. It was not looking safe, as every known or half-known retreat would not be safe now. As a group of sharers were going at the end of the month, they would arrange Tommy to go with them.

Tommy longed to tell them the truth, but any time he tried to even half bring it up, they silenced him, with it was his own business and anyhow, it would be a burden to them to know any more. Jock said he would buy a ticket and get cash from the bank he owed Tommy. Tommy thanked him graciously, and again he wished to tell him the truth of why he was on the run, but each time he opened his mouth to tell Jock, he waved his hand and, *"The less I know the better, question not asked or no question answered."* Of course, Jock had lived here for going on forty years.

Learning the Truth

On his return from Shannon Airport, twenty years been gone, Michael John slumped down upon the leather chair, not wanting to hear any more sad news this day. So gripping the two arms of the chair, he said to the old man, *"Go ahead, tell me about Tommy,"* as he put his third whiskey to his mouth and drank.

"Well it was a long time ago as you know, Michael John. I, myself, was a young, well maybe not so young, but a dynamic man even if I say to myself. I thought I could get to the bottom of any case at that time. That case did puzzle me; I never thought for a moment young Tommy had anything to do with the killing. As it turns out, she was his mother. From all the stories about those who held hatred of Hugh was well known, a week before at the Macra dinner in the Clews Hall, when asked about Hugh, he was cutting a piece of meat and he laughed saying, I wish that was him, as he chopped at it viciously, lots of stories in the same vein.

"Well, a warrant was put out for the arrest, the first place they went for port was Cobh, but we knew he never boarded it. There was a very intense search, the greatest man hunt since the beginning of the Free State. Even the church was involved, as he was reared in the convent. It was said the nuns were too easy on the boys in their care. It was the end of children taken into care in that particular convent."

Michael John lifted his head, *"I always knew, since Tommy was nine and a bit, he was living with his parents. He told me the very next day he found out himself, but begged me to keep silent. Sure wasn't that why he wanted to go away and make a home, so his mother would have some peace for the end of her days; she was not short of money. It was shortly before we left, he told me his mother had quite a stash of money; she showed Tommy where it was and gave him a large sum. He said he would not be short till we were earning.*

Well the solicitor hung his head then and went on to say that every piece of evidence seemed against him. *No one stood up very much, although quite a few said they could not believe but had no proof. It seemed everyone that could have helped him were gone or afraid to come forward. His aunt and uncle in England would not come forward with his true identity, because they thought it might make him look guilty then. If old Murray had not dominated his house with rods of iron and delusions of grandeur, it is no wonder they nicknamed him the half Sir. Jimmy Joe was not so terrified of his father running him out of the house if he told about his widow. Mind you, there was no loss on the widow, sure was not from good enough people and then her being a widow with no family – sure she was barren – old Murray would laugh about her. Some people say he threw his own hat in, but she threw it out after him. Now old Murray never knew anything about this, of course. No one seemed to want to get on the wrong side of old Murray, sure didn't he have two horses and a nice few pieces of machinery. He also has this canvas cover; any neighbour building a reek of hay would be very pleased to borrow it in case it would rain. He also had a cousin in a rope factory; he would bring old Murray ropes at the right price – another treasure to have – that was shared by the neighbourhood for tying down the house in case of a storm or the pikes of hay. He was kind enough with his possessions so long as folk looked up to him. When he did come forward to clear Tommy, we could not find him to tell him he was a free man. No one knows if he is dead or alive. If he went somehow to Australia, the only job Tommy would have got was fencing the barbed wire across the state. Sure he must never have come back; he worked for weeks*

85

without seeing anyone. A plane dropped materials and food every six weeks; if anyone got ill and died, they were just buried along by the ditches. It was big money but very dangerous, but if one had no trade, it would be the most likely job they would have got. That is if he ever got there at all. It was like as if he was swallowed up." Getting up slowly from the chair, the old solicitor, his face racked in pain from arthritis, putting his hand forward to shake Michael John's hand, said, *"I think we will leave it there today, come in tomorrow or whenever feels like, I will see you about your father's will and your aunt's insurance. Go and have a rest. Your father left a few wishes and other small items for you to see to, but till we meet again, good luck, son."*

Silence of Snow

Michael John thought to himself it was time to retrace some steps. Getting out of the car at the end of the boheen, he felt the enchantment of night, walking under a winter's moon on a sparkling, frosty, snow-covered earth. *'The silence of not being able to hear your own feet in the snow as you trudge along, as if the world belonged to you alone,'* Michael John thought to himself as he looked towards the planting that had been sown since he had left.

The evergreens standing there, casting their regal shadows upon the crisp earth, as if keeping the rest of the world at a distance, a fox's shrill bark in rapid yelps hits like an electric current bolting through his brain. *'Yes,'* he thought, it is his world too; this path has soaked up as much animal's blood as human's, as any spot anywhere on earth. Every other sphere of life had changed beyond belief around the old home place. Not so the moonlight, Michael John wondered, given by the majestic moon suspended between heaven and earth, towering so distinctively apart from the rest of the world that not even time could touch it.

As he came to the head of the pass, he could see the white-washed cottage nestled within the circle of large gnarled ash trees, the top branches wrapped around each other as if as they were trying to hide their secrets. The plain windows, like wide-open eyes, searching for its master to return again. This path he was walking again, after twenty years of being an immigrant in America.

Long ago, he spent every moment he could spare with Tommy and his foster mother; he was the one youngster the tyrant could stand around the place. Then each Saturday night, he would call for Tommy in his father's old Prefect car, and off they would go dancing with the gang to the Silver Slipper in Strandhill. In the midst of all returning memories, Michael remembered to himself the night Tommy said to his foster father after working hard all week that he had not the price of a stamp while standing at the doorway ready to go; the tyrant put his hand into his pocket and handed him three pence.

Standing by the orchid gate, he looked to the left where once held tiny vegetable gardens, one inside the other. Here he toiled many a springs' day helping Tommy. His foster father was a tyrant of a man; it was no wonder he was nick named 'tyrant'. If he could not find a job for Tommy, he would take the gate down and have him stand in the gap all day keeping the cattle in. It was always open season on hatred when Hugh Drury was near.

Looking to the right, nothing seemed to have changed; the old ruins of the ancient nunnery with its graveyard weather-eroded headstones that stood at all angles, some completely wrapped in ivy. Turning back to the cottage, he remembered all the winter nights he spent inside in that kitchen. Nelly, Tommy's foster mother, taught them how to play the tin whistle. Oh could she make it talk when we did our best to learn, as one at a time kept our vigil at the window, keeping a weary look out for the tyrant, as he hated music or any entertainment with a vengeance! Well at least when it was in his house. He could not bear to see Tommy relax. He would have a heap of old ropes under the stairs up to the loft or a bag hay to make ropes. There was an old butter box that was full of all kind of nails and screws to select them together into little brown parcels, then to write the kind and size on the outside.

Needless to say, Tommy hit off to a rambling house at nightfall after he had eaten supper. The only hobby he allowed Tommy was to go fishing on a dark summer's day, as he knew all the good feeding spots. Mind you, Tommy's fishing rod consisted of a piece of string, a safety pin and an old Guinness cork. He often caught thirty perch in an hour of course – there was some eating in that.

Michael John's job was to keep his eyes peeled to see when the flash lamp shone towards the sky, as that meant the tyrant was binding down to open the wooden gate at the road, coming home from rambling in his cousin Joe's house. Now Joe Kielty was the grandest man on God's good earth, he could see no wrong in anybody, he made excuses for every man's failing. He would say people never were bad and that they couldn't help it. Or in the tyrant case, ah! Sure he has got a dose of the atmospherics.

Standing there, feeling an eerie sense of foreboding surrounding him, he tried to walk away. Then his eyes reverted to the flickering light in the doorway. *"Oh Nelly,"* he said to himself, feeling really pleased to see her. She shuffled out on her right leg, as it was longer than the other. What's that tune she's playing, it is the 'Derry Air'. Oh what heavenly sweet music. Looking, he sees there is nothing but fresh air between her fingers. His neck prickles with fear, as he was about to call out to her. Holding his head, as if his mind was leaving his skull, he tried to move.

'I must be going mad,' he thought to himself as he stumbled down the path. *"Too much sorrowful sad news in one day must be getting to me,"* he said to himself. Poor Nelly left this world, rather she was pushed out of it the same day he had left Irish soil to sail for America. *'If only one could go ahead in life and flush out the bad things,'* he thought, feeling there was no moisture left in his soul. He wished deeply to see Tommy again, his childhood friend and soul mate. Oh they are an awful lot of ifs and buts in this life; if his uncle had not been in a car crash as he were crossing the Atlantic.

On arriving, he not only couldn't recognise him, he did not know of such a person. There was nothing else to do but look for other lodgings elsewhere with the help of his uncle's wife. He lodged with a couple second generation Irish; they were very kind to him and helped him get work. It was supposed to be for a short period, but as everyone was happy with the arrangements, he was still living there till the day he returned home. Never hearing a word from the day he left home, he could not understand Aunt Maggie had even sent him off with the stamped addressed envelopes. Well that was another thing he had learnt today.

On the day he left, when Aunt Maggie retuned from Knock, she went straight to bed as she could not sleep the night before, thinking her Michael John was leaving, although she had encouraged him; it was like a part of herself had died. So taking a large hot whiskey, something she did not indulge in often and a Beechams powder, she finally went to sleep.

It was well bright the next morning, and the hens were clucking outside the back door when she awoke. She got up and dressed; she went to get some breakfast when she found some porridge made. It seemed Paul had got up early and gone to the bog. It was about 10 o'clock when Flute Lavin called, looking for some duck eggs she usually kept for him, then didn't he up and tell her the terrible news. She then heard the bad news about the brutal murders of the Drurys, and of how they were looking for Tommy, of how he was nowhere to be found. On top of Mickey, who she loved as deeply, as if she had given birth to him herself, leaving that day before. They told him how she got some kind of weakness and lost the power of speech, and all down her left side was useless. All the neighbours had helped Paul in every way to take care of her, as everyone held her in high regard.

Regardless of the help and encouragement, she slowly melted away, without saying a word; she left this world for the next, on the night before Christmas. It was very sad, as Maggie loved her flowers and kept her little garden looking beautiful. Yet the only display of flora was a single twig of red-berried holly on top of the coffin. Needless to say, it took its toll on his father, he just seemed to deteriorate from the time the two people he had in his world had left him.

Though he struggled on for another five years before he took his final departure, no one could in get touch with him. Well he said didn't he send five of her self-addressed envelopes, but he never got any answer and as missed her so much, it was easier to pretend to forget.

As time went on, he intended to return but kept putting it off. As both his father and Aunt Maggie were both reasonable young people, he never thought there was any rush.

Now all this grief and bad news he heard today, could his head be ever right again; this thought choked within his brain.

Not to mention Mary Agnes – oh how she so loved Tommy and he returned this affection, he had told me sure, he would send for her as well. Although Mary Agnes was not a raving beauty, she did have a beauty of her own, a kind and gentle lass she was indeed. She worked to help her father out as well. *'I will go and see the two of them, I know it is late,'* he thought to himself, *'but sure I will tell them I would not be able to rest the night, if I do not see a friendly face.'* So off he drove up the boheen, the light seemed brighter than it used to be or sure they must have got the electricity.

He thought to himself as he pulled up on the front street, the door opened and light poured out getting out of the car, he shuffled to stand up. As he walked towards the door, you could hear his boots vibrating off the stones. There in the corner with the tongs in her hand to pull some sods up on the sad-looking fire, she looked up dropping the tongs on to the ashes, she lets out this strange straggling sound and jumps up looking at Michael John's face.

He rambled on saying, *"I only found out all this day or the last twenty four hours, oh Mary Agnes,"* as she flung her arms around his neck as if she was about to choke him.

When letting go, she cried, *"It is so good to see you. We had been inseparable and had such a great childhood didn't we all hang together. What can we do for Tommy, no one wanted to help him, only the Lees; they were his real family."*

"Yes, I always knew, we did not tell you because you were a girl, that was the only reason."

Mary Agnes shook back her head as if in mock annoyance, then went on to tell him, *"When I heard your car, I thought it was my cousin Moira, whom is five years younger than me; she stays on with me for company during the winter months, since Dad died eight years ago on the fifteenth of August. He always cursed immigration; he said things would never have turned out this way if the lads had only stayed at home. He reckoned none of ye would ever have gone hungry and with Rafferty draining of the river, was not there plenty of work. And do you know I always said my father was a wise man, he was right in that as well.*

"Do you know what, you will you sleep here the night, actually I will pull out the settle bed and ready it then. I will get some of that fresh bread and some cooked meat, then we will crack a bottle of whiskey and when Moira comes in, she will meet you. Then after a good night's sleep, we will start making plans of how to find Tommy," and they clapped the back of each other's hands like they did as kids. With light steps, one opened the bottle, the other got out the glasses, as he knew where everything was in this house and Mary E sliced away at the soda cake.